DANGER ON VAMPIRE TRAIL

An assignment from their famous detective father to track down a ring of credit-card counterfeiters takes Frank and Joe Hardy on an exciting camping trip to the Rocky Mountains.

The cross-country trek with their pals Chet Morton and Biff Hooper is jinxed from the very first day. Trouble with their tent trailer is compounded by vicious harassments all the way to Colorado. Here their enemies strike at Biff's lovable bloodhound in another attempt to scare the teen-age detectives off the case. In Denver a skein of clues confuses the Hardys. How many gangs are out to get them—one, two, or three?

Strange happenings on a nearly impassable mountain lure Frank, Joe, Chet, and Biff to almost certain death before they discover the sinister reason for the danger on Vampire Trail.

Frank saw the robed figure of a man

Hardy Boys Mystery Stories

DANGER ON VAMPIRE TRAIL

BY

FRANKLIN W. DIXON

GROSSET & DUNLAP

Publishers • New York

CONTENTS

DANGER ON
VAMPIRE TRAIL

CHAPTER I

Sporty Swindlers

"Do you boys feel up to tackling a counterfeit case?" Detective Fenton Hardy asked his sons. He looked at eighteen-year-old, dark-haired Frank and then at blond, seventeen-year-old Joe. They were seated in comfortable leather chairs in their famous father's study.

Frank grinned. "Of course, Dad! We'll tackle anything from flying fullbacks to dangerous crooks. What's the scoop?"

"A strange one," Mr. Hardy replied. "A gang is counterfeiting the famous Magnacard."

"The so-called millionaire's charge card?"

"Yes. No questions asked on purchases or ready cash up to ten thousand dollars."

"How can we help?" Joe wanted to know.

"By taking over the entire assignment. I've been asked to handle a high-priority case for the government."

1

Frank and Joe had assisted their father in solving many cases. The first one was the mystery of *The Tower Treasure,* and in their most recent caper, *The Bombay Boomerang,* the boys had saved Mr. Hardy's life.

The responsibility of a sleuthing job always gave Frank and Joe a tingling of excitement.

"Well?" Fenton Hardy said, his lips curling into a slow smile. "Anyone interested?"

Joe blurted, "You know we are!"

"When do we start?" Frank said.

"In a few days. But it'll involve a camping trip."

"Camping! That's right up our alley, Dad." Joe got up and paced around. "Chet's been bugging us to go on a camping trip for a long time."

"He sure has," Frank agreed. "Chet wants to get a trailer tent, but he's short of cash."

Mr. Hardy said, "We might work something out. Expense money, perhaps. Then there's a possibility of the reward."

"What reward?" Frank asked.

Mr. Hardy explained that a very rich man, who had been duped by the counterfeiters, had posted a reward of two thousand dollars for their capture and conviction.

"Wow!" said Joe, grinning.

Realizing the importance of the exciting mission, the boys became serious. "Tell us all about the case, Dad," Frank urged. "What's the M.O. in this new racket?"

The modus operandi was one of the first lessons in criminal psychology Mr. Hardy had taught his sons. Habit, the boys knew, had been the downfall of many thieves, who plied their nefarious trade in the same manner every time they committed a crime.

Mr. Hardy said, "The swindlers apparently got hold of Magnacard's master file—important data on all the clients, including copies of their signatures. They duplicated the credit cards perfectly, then forged identification papers—drivers' licenses and the like. They purchase goods which are then billed to the owner of the charge card."

"A lot of rich men must be pulling their hair out, getting all these bills!"

"To say the least. It's up to you to keep them from getting absolutely bald!"

Joe asked, "But why the camping trip? How does that come into the picture?"

"I've been waiting for you to ask that," Mr. Hardy replied. He lifted a sheaf of papers from his desk drawer. "The counterfeiters have been operating mostly in the Rocky Mountains area, although there have been some incidents in the Midwest, and the East, too."

The detective sat back, fingers locked behind his head, while his sons examined the dossier. Then a quick look of enlightenment crossed Frank's face. "Hey, Joe. I see it! These guys have been using the Magnacards to buy sporting equipment."

"Exactly," Mr. Hardy said. "They purchase motorboats, motorcycles, tents—you name it. Then they sell the merchandise lower than the retail price."

Joe remarked, "To suckers who are unaware they're getting hot goods. Or to dishonest, greedy people who are more interested in buying something cheap, regardless of whether the deal is on the level or not."

The detective nodded and pulled a small photograph from his pocket. "Here's a prime suspect," he said. The boys leaned over the desk to look at it.

"Pretty fuzzy picture," Joe remarked.

Frank said, "Probably a blowup from a small negative. Right, Dad?"

"That's it. An amateur photographer took it by chance after one of the swindlers had borrowed five thousand dollars from a bank and was coming out the front door."

The young detectives studied every detail of the photograph. The face was round, with a low, black hairline. The eyes were far apart. The mouth was small and turned up at the corners in a puckish grin. The general appearance was that of a short man in his thirties.

At that moment the trio were startled by a scream from downstairs.

"It's Aunt Gertrude!" Frank exclaimed. He

bounded from the room, with Joe at his heels. They scrambled down the stairs and rushed into the kitchen. Their aunt was pointing a snaking hand at the window. Her jaws moved, but no words passed her lips.

Instantly Frank and Joe, as well as Fenton Hardy, who had followed them, saw the cause of the woman's fright. A huge hound dog was looking through the window screen. Aunt Gertrude, after recovering from her shock, told them that she had been seated at the kitchen table, deep in thought. Turning her head, she suddenly had looked straight into the sad droopy eyes of the Peeping Tom dog.

Joe started to chuckle. "It's Biff Hooper's blood-hound, Auntie! He wouldn't hurt a flea."

"Don't laugh!" she scolded.

"I'm not laughing," Joe said. "But it was so funny—"

"Not funny, either!" snorted Miss Hardy.

Frank turned his head away, knowing that Aunt Gertrude's wrath would be further aroused if she detected the faintest trace of a grin on his face.

Mr. Hardy said, "Well, that crisis is over," and went upstairs to his study.

His sister had come to live with Mr. and Mrs. Hardy and their two sons several years ago. Beneath her stern manner, she was extremely fond of the boys. Gertrude Hardy had never approved of her brother's daring exploits when he was a detective in the New York City Police Department, nor was she outwardly impressed by the international reputation he had acquired as a private investigator.

"Too dangerous, too risky," she always said.

When her nephews followed in their father's footsteps, Aunt Gertrude was even more forceful in her warnings.

Frank and Joe realized that their safety was her chief concern, and that her heart was really soft as the fluffy meringue on top of her famous lemon pies.

Meanwhile, the dog had padded around to the kitchen door. A voice called:

"Sherlock! Come here!" Biff Hooper, a tall blond boy, appeared, bent down and snapped a leather leash on the hound's collar. He looped the end over the outside doorknob and entered.

"Hiya, guys," he said breezily. "Just taking old Sherlock on a training exercise and he got away from me. Headed right for the Hardy home. Are you baking pie today, Aunt Gertrude?"

"I was going to," Miss Hardy replied, "until that beast frightened me!"

"Don't mind him," Biff said and straddled a kitchen chair. "He's harmless."

Biff Hooper was a six-foot, broad-shouldered athlete—big and powerful as a football lineman, fast and hard-hitting as a boxer. But his usual

A huge hound was looking through the screen

good-natured smile was missing now, and the Hardys sensed that he had a problem.

"What's up, Biff? You look worried," Frank said.

"Something wrong?" asked Joe.

"Could be." Biff hesitated, and Aunt Gertrude stepped out of the kitchen, realizing the boys wanted to talk in private. "It's about Chet," Biff added.

Chet Morton, the Hardy boys' closest friend, lived on a farm on the outskirts of Bayport. He was on the high school's grid squad by virtue of his ample bulk, which could plug a hole in the team's forward wall like a truck. Neither Frank nor Joe had seen Chet in several days.

"What's the matter?" Frank prodded. "Did something happen to Chet?"

"Oh no," Biff replied. "At least not yet."

"What do you mean?"

"Maybe I'm imagining things," Biff said with a frown. "But I noticed Chet coming out of the bank—"

"You think he robbed it?" Joe quipped.

"Don't be an idiot," Biff retorted. "I saw him coming out of the bank holding an envelope—I mean *clutching* it!"

"Go on," Frank urged.

"So I said, 'What do you have there, Chet? The key to Fort Knox?' "

"What did he say?" Joe asked.

"He wouldn't tell me anything," Biff replied. "Chet seemed awful mysterious. He looked up and down the street and hurried off to his jalopy. I thought you fellows ought to know about it, seeing you're such buddies."

Joe said, "Do you think someone's after Chet's hard-earned money?"

"Possibly."

Just then the phone rang. Joe picked up the kitchen extension. . . . "Chet? We were just talking about you!"

The voice on the other end was curt. "Joe, I haven't got time to gab."

"How come?"

"Never mind. I've got to see you and Frank right away."

"Where are you?"

"Home."

"We'll come right over."

Joe hung up and turned to the others. "Your hunch seems to be right, Biff. I think Chet's in trouble. Let's go, Frank!"

CHAPTER II

About Face!

AFTER bidding good-by to Biff, the Hardys jumped into their car. Minutes later they arrived at the Morton farm and drove up to the comfortable rambling house.

As they parked, a dark-haired, pixie-like girl came to the door. She was Iola Morton, Joe's "special friend." She and Joe often double-dated with Frank and his girl friend, Callie Shaw.

"Why the frowns?" Iola said breezily as she hooked an arm through Joe's.

"We think your brother's in trouble," Frank said. "He phoned us to come out."

Iola laughed. "That was just a trick to get you here in a hurry. He's over there behind the barn," she said, pointing.

"I'm glad to hear he's okay," Joe said, "but I ought to sock him for worrying us!" He and Frank trotted around the barn. To their amazement, they saw Chet standing beside a brand-new trailer tent. It was opened up and ready for occupancy.

"That's a beauty!" Frank said. "Where'd you get it, Chet?"

"And where'd you get the green stuff to buy it?" Joe asked. "This outfit's worth more than a thousand bucks!"

Chet beamed. "One question at a time," he said with a matter-of-fact air. "First, let me show you around this camper paradise."

Frank and Joe stepped inside. The smell of newness pervaded the air, and the interior was bright and spotless. Fold-out arms of the compact little trailer provided two bunks, sleeping four. Other facilities included a lavatory, refrigerator, and a three-burner gas stove.

"Chet, this is simply the greatest!" Joe exulted. "How did you know that Frank and I were going on a camping trip?"

"Cut it out," Chet replied. "I've been trying to persuade you for a long time. Thought I'd take the bull by the horns and do something about it."

"Honest," Frank said. "We *are* going on a trip."

Chet's eyes narrowed. "Business or pleasure?"

"Business primarily," Frank replied. "Dad's given us a new case."

"When I go camping," Chet said, "I want to go for fun. None of this dangerous detective stuff."

"But we'd chip in expense money," Joe said. "Dad would help finance us."

"And then there's the two-thousand-dollar reward," Frank said evenly, watching Chet's face for a reaction.

Chet's eyebrows shot up.

"There's a reward for catching some credit-card counterfeiters," Frank explained.

"Where do we go?"

"Out West."

"Now you're talking!" Chet said, putting a hefty arm around Frank's shoulder.

As they stepped out of the camper, Joe said, "Chet, where'd you buy this? And if you don't mind my asking, how much?"

The stout boy put one foot on the trailer step and assumed an attitude of casual superiority. "My astute business acumen," he said, "culminated in a most beneficial purchase."

"Come on," Joe said, annoyed by Chet's pretentious air. "Give us the straight facts."

"All right. To put it in language you understand, I put an ad in the newspaper and landed a great bargain."

"Go on," Frank prodded.

"A man came to me," Chet said, "and offered this beauty at a reduced price. After he had purchased it, his wife became ill and their camping trip was called off."

"What do you call a reduced price?" Frank asked.

"How about four hundred dollars?" Chet replied, arching his eyebrows.

"Wow!" Joe exclaimed. "That's a steal!"

"Was everything legal?" Frank wanted to know, recalling what his father had told them about the credit-card gang.

"All in order," Chet assured the boys. "I'll get my plates tomorrow."

Joe laughed and told Chet how Biff had seen him coming from the bank with the money.

"Sure, I was holding onto it tight," Chet said. "That four hundred dollars was my entire fortune." He added, "Hey, maybe Biff would like to come along, too!"

"It's your camper," Frank said. "Why don't you invite him?"

Chet said he would, and the Hardys departed for home. Mrs. Hardy, who had been out shopping, was delighted to hear of their plans. "Be sure to take your heavy sweaters, and raincoats, and—"

"Our rubbers," Joe finished the sentence.

"Of course not," Laura Hardy said with a pretty smile. "I was about to say take your waterproof boots."

As Mrs. Hardy and Aunt Gertrude busied themselves preparing dinner, the boys told their father of the camping plans. "If Biff can go, it'll really beef up our forces," Joe concluded.

Later that evening Biff Hooper phoned. "I think I can join you on that trip, Frank. But I'll have to bring my hound along." Biff explained that he had been training the bloodhound and did not want to break the routine.

"Not a bad idea," Frank said. "Having a dog named Sherlock on a detective case might bring us luck."

Preparations for their trip occupied the Hardys and their friends for the next two days. Frank and Joe had installed a trailer hitch on their car and had gone to Chet's house to pick up the camper.

The outfit presented a sleek silhouette, low enough for the driver to have clear vision to the rear.

On the morning of departure the Hardy family got up at five o'clock. At six Biff arrived with the sad-eyed hound and got in the back seat with Chet. Frank took the wheel and Joe sat alongside of him. With shouts of good-by and wishes of good luck from the elder Hardys, the quartet set off.

Fenton Hardy had briefed his sons the night before. He wanted them to check out sports resorts in the Rocky Mountains area for evidence of Magnacard swindles and try to track down the perpetrators. They were also to quiz merchants who had been duped. Their father had given them a typed list of the dealers' names and addresses.

As they drove out of town, Joe remarked, "I wish we had more concrete clues to start with."

"Hah!" said Chet. "If I know you guys, you'll fall into a mess of them soon enough!"

The day was pleasant and traffic was light at that early hour. The car hummed along, with the camper gliding behind. Frank followed Shore Road for several miles until it joined a superhighway leading west. The speed limit was higher, so Frank accelerated.

The boys were about fifty miles from Bayport when they heard the wailing of a siren.

"You've got a heavy foot," Biff said to Frank. "Must have gone over the speed limit."

Chet moaned. "Here's trouble even before we get started!"

A trooper moved alongside and motioned Frank to pull over to the shoulder. Frank complied, then stepped out of the car. The officer, who had parked up ahead, strode up to him.

"What's the trouble, sir?" Frank asked.

"Let's see your license and registration."

Frank pulled out the papers. The trooper studied them, then eyed the camper. "Do you own this?" he asked Frank.

"No. Our friend Chet Morton does."

"Where is he?"

"Right here, Officer," Chet said, getting out. The dog yelped as Chet stepped on his foot in the process.

"We weren't speeding, were we?" Frank inquired.

"No."

"But then why—?"

"It's the trailer I'm interested in. I'll have to take you back to Bayport."

"You must be kidding!" Joe exclaimed. "What's the charge?"

"Possession of stolen property."

"Stolen property!" Chet exclaimed. "But I paid cash for this!"

"Tell that to the police captain." The trooper gave Chet a suspicious look, then ordered Frank to turn about and follow him.

For several miles they traveled in glum silence. Finally Frank said, "I thought you got the camper pretty cheap, Chet."

There was no reply. Chet was crushed by the thought of losing his bank account and of being involved in a shady deal.

Biff tried to be helpful. "I don't think they can arrest you, Chet. You were an innocent victim."

Finally Chet spoke. "Am I stupid!" he muttered, then sat silent again.

The trooper pulled into the State Police barracks on the outskirts of Bayport. Chet was interrogated by the captain in charge.

When the boy had finished his story, a man was called in from an adjoining room. He was introduced as George Browning, owner of the Bayport Sports Equipment Company. The Hardys had heard of him. Mr. Browning identified the trailer tent as the one he had sold to a man who had given his name as Cyrus Kogan.

Chet perked up immediately. "That's the man I got it from. Isn't that perfectly legal?"

"Kogan bought the goods with a fake credit card," Browning replied. "One of those counterfeit Magnacards!"

The Hardys were thunderstruck. A fake Magnacard operator in Bayport! Frank pulled out his wallet and showed the photo clue to Chet and the merchant.

Both identified the man as Kogan!

Biff said, "This crook's been under your nose right in town, fellows!"

The camper was left at the police barracks. Mr. Browning refused to press any charges against Chet, and even offered to sell him the camper at a reduced price because it was now considered a used one.

When the boys returned home, the elder Hardys were shocked and dismayed to learn of the discouraging turn of events. They all consoled Chet, and much to the relief of. Frank and Joe, Aunt Gertrude did not say "I told you so." Instead, she offered to bake him any kind of pie he desired.

"Humble pie," Chet said, downcast.

"Now you just erase that long face, Chester," Aunt Gertrude said. "You'll have a deep-dish apple pie tomorrow!"

That afternoon the Hardy boys and their father

went to Bayport Police Headquarters to have a conference with Chief Collig. He was a ruddy-faced man, who cooperated fully with the detective and his sons whenever they were working on a case.

"I was sorry to lower the boom on Chet," he said, "but it was my duty to notify the State Police of any trailer tents I saw around Bayport."

The chief explained that he had warned merchants to beware of the fake Cyrus Kogan. "However," Collig added, "I think he's skipped town by now."

Mr. Hardy spoke up. "Bayport's a pretty big place with many shops, Chief. I think the guy might hang around to swindle another dealer or two. His success at Browning's may feed his ego."

The boys agreed with their father and laid a plan to catch the criminal. That evening they called their friends together. Chet and Biff came over, along with Tony Prito and Phil Cohen. Tony was a handsome boy with an olive complexion. Phil was a slight youth and an A-student in Bayport High.

When they had all gathered in the living room, Frank outlined the plan. They would stake out the stores in Bayport where expensive merchandise was sold.

"We'll watch fur shops, fancy jewelers, and the like," Frank said. He showed the boys the picture of Kogan, and Chet added whatever description he could. "The guy's as smooth as maple syrup," he concluded.

The stakeout the next day produced nothing but tired feet and boredom as the weary boys watched in vain.

On the second day, while Frank and Joe were home for lunch, Phil Cohen phoned, his voice edged with excitement.

"What's up, Phil?" Joe asked.

"I saw him, Joe!"

"Where?"

"He went into the Corner Antique Shop."

"Okay. Keep an eye on him. Frank and I will be right over."

Joe flipped his napkin on the table, grabbed the car keys, and ran out. Frank followed.

"I hope we get him!" Frank said, sliding into the seat next to the driver. "But it means the end of our camping trip!"

"Don't be too sure about that," Joe said. "He's not the only Magnacard swindler. And he might not talk!"

Minutes later Joe parked at a prudent distance from the shop, located near a residential area north of town.

The shop was housed in a rustic cottage which lent an aura of antiquity to the establishment. There was only one car in sight, parked halfway down the block. As they approached the shop, Frank and Joe saw Phil flattened against the wall next to the front door. He motioned them to be silent.

The Hardys slithered up beside Phil and listened. Frank put one eye to the edge of an open window. The customer, whom Frank identified immediately as their man, was examining an antique rifle.

"This one is rather expensive," the shopkeeper said. "It's extremely rare!"

"Rare guns are my hobby," the customer replied. With that Kogan pulled out his wallet and produced a credit card.

"Ah, a Magnacard," the shopkeeper said, smiling.

"Oh nuts!" Frank thought. "This dealer hasn't been warned." To his brother and Phil he said, "Come on."

They walked in quietly but the man heard them. As he wheeled around, the Hardys made a dive for him. But Kogan was agile. He swung the rifle, hitting both boys across the chest.

Frank and Joe cried out in pain and fell to the floor.

CHAPTER III

Farewell Party

TERRIFIED, the shopkeeper ducked down behind the counter. The man, still carrying the gun, dashed past Phil, jabbed the boy with the muzzle and knocked him off balance. Then he raced outside, sprinted halfway down the block, and jumped into the car which the boys had noticed before. Seconds later he roared off.

The Hardys were stunned by the painful wallop, but they recovered quickly. Joe dashed to the phone to call the police, while Frank ran outside with Phil. Although too late to stop the swindler, they got the license number of the getaway car.

The shopkeeper, meanwhile, was bemoaning the loss of the antique rifle. "You'd think if he's rich enough to have a Magnacard, he'd pay for the merchandise!" he said.

Joe told him that the credit card was probably

a fake and briefly explained about the counterfeit operation.

"I won't accept any more of those Magnacards," the man said as Frank scoured the shop for possible clues.

"Look at this!" Frank exclaimed. He bent down to pick up a loafer-type shoe which apparently had fallen off as the fugitive ran out. The quality of the leather and the workmanship were superb. The label read: *Mountain Dogies*.

"Evidently our crook buys nothing but the best," Joe remarked.

"Did you ever hear of this brand?" Phil asked.

"No, but we can check it out," Frank replied.

Two policemen arrived a few minutes later. The boys reported all they knew, then followed the officers back to headquarters where they talked with Chief Collig.

The swindler's license number was quickly checked out. It proved to be that of a car stolen the day before from a Bayport parking lot.

"And here's the shoe the fellow lost," Frank said. "There might be fingerprints on the shiny part of the leather, Chief."

The department's fingerprint expert was called. He lifted several prints, and Collig dispatched them immediately to the FBI via wirephoto. The Hardys thanked Phil for his good detective work, then went home to take hot baths to relieve their bruised ribs.

Early the next morning Collig phoned. "We know the identity of that swindler," he told Frank. "Thanks to the fingerprints on his shoe."

"Who is he, Chief?"

"Archibald Lasher. His nickname is Whip."

Collig ticked off Whip Lasher's record. "It includes several bunco raps, mail fraud, and automobile thefts."

"But here's something interesting in his profile," the chief went on. "He's a great outdoorsman—very fond of camping. And he's a practical joker."

"Could you send us a copy of his dossier?" Frank asked. The chief promised he would and hung up.

"Well, Dad," Frank said, after relaying Collig's information to his father and Joe, "what do you think Lasher will do next?"

"My guess is that he'll lie low for a while."

"Do you still want us to go west?" asked Joe.

"Certainly. Lasher is only one of the gang. Besides, I wouldn't be surprised if he headed west right away."

Then the detective proposed lending the boys money to put a down payment on Chet's ill-fated camper.

"That would be great, Dad!" Joe said, and immediately phoned the good news to Chet and Biff.

Next day Frank, Joe, and Chet made arrangements with Mr. Browning to purchase the trailer tent. The dealer cut the price drastically and allowed plenty of time to complete payment.

Before returning home, the Hardys went to police headquarters and talked to Collig. He told the boys that Mountain Dogies shoes were sold exclusively in the huge Mountain Dogie sporting goods store in Denver.

"All clues point west," Frank mused. "Could we have the inner sole of that shoe, Chief?"

"I don't see why not," Collig replied. "What are you going to do with it?"

"Give Lasher a hot-foot!" Frank joked.

The chief had one of his men cut out the inner sole and handed it to Frank.

"Hope it helps," Collig said. "When are you leaving?"

"Tomorrow morning."

"Incidentally," Collig said, "we found the getaway car abandoned. I don't think we'll see Whip Lasher around here any more, not after that close escape yesterday."

"Good," Joe said. "Then we can have a farewell party in peace!"

That evening the four travelers along with Tony and Phil gathered at the Hardy home. All the boys brought dates. Joe played the guitar while his friends sang and danced. There was plenty of good food, topped off by Aunt Gertrude's pies.

"One thing you must take with you is your guitar," Callie Shaw told Joe.

"Out on the prairie," Iola said laughingly, "you can sing sad songs and dream of us, pining for you at home."

"Not on your life," Biff remarked. "We'll be busy tracking down the crooks."

"That's why we're bringing Sherlock along," Frank said. "Once he picks up Whip Lasher's trail there'll be no stopping him!"

Mrs. Hardy looked in on the young people to see if their food supply was ample.

"Joe tells me you're having a birthday soon, Mrs. Hardy," Callie called out.

"Oh, no one was supposed to know about that!" Laura Hardy replied shyly. "But Frank and Joe never forget the day."

"What would you like for a present, Mother? Maybe we can buy it on our trip," Frank said.

"I always wanted a sapphire birthstone from the West," Mrs. Hardy replied. She said that her great-grandfather had been a pioneer in the Rockies. Just then the front doorbell rang and Phil quipped, "Maybe the neighbors called the police to put a lid on the noise."

The man standing at the door was dressed in a messenger's uniform. He quickly handed an envelope to Mrs. Hardy, then hurried off.

"Fenton!" she called out. "It's for you!"

The detective came downstairs, took the envelope, and opened it. Inside was a Magnacard made out in his name.

Chet chuckled. "Now you can take your wife on an around-the-world trip—on the cuff, Mr. Hardy."

"Didn't you say Whip Lasher is a practical joker?" Mr. Hardy asked Frank.

"Chief Collig did," Frank replied.

"Well, I think this is one of Lasher's tricks. No doubt this card is a counterfeit."

As the party broke up, the young people thanked Mrs. Hardy and Aunt Gertrude for helping to make it such an enjoyable evening.

Before setting out the next morning the campers checked to be sure they had packed everything. Their equipment included a collapsible rubber boat, a small outboard motor, campers' guidebooks and maps and their two-way radio.

Tony and Phil came to say good-by, and with much horn-tooting the four started off for the second time. Sherlock sensed the excitement, and yapped a couple of times as the car and trailer turned the corner and disappeared from sight.

Frank stayed at the wheel for three hours, then changed places with Joe. Bayport lay far behind and the road stretched ahead like an undulating ribbon.

Biff played his harmonica for a while, but quit when Sherlock started to howl.

"You're hurting his ears," Chet said, "and mine, too!"

"Okay," Biff said. "Joe and I will give you a concert tonight."

The car was climbing a long hill when Joe decided to pull out and pass a slow-moving truck. Coming in the opposite direction was another vehicle. But it was far enough away to give Joe time to pass. He stepped on the gas, but did not get as much speed as he expected.

"Oh man! I forgot about our trailer," Joe said. "It's heavier than I thought."

The Hardys' convertible was nearly parallel to the truck's cab. The oncoming vehicle loomed larger by the second. Joe was in a dilemma. Should he press forward or fall back? Either way was risky. In the back seat Biff and Chet froze. Frank offered no advice, Joe would have to make the decision himself.

He floored the accelerator, the car crawled past the truck, then he cut sharply to the right. The truck driver put on his brakes and the other car zipped past with only inches to spare.

Looking back Chet saw that the camper, tilted on one wheel, had barely cleared the truck's front bumper.

Everybody exhaled in relief at the same time. No one spoke for a few minutes. Then Joe remarked sheepishly, "From now on I won't forget we're towing a trailer."

To ease the tension, Biff pulled out his harmonica again and played for a few minutes until Sherlock howled for a halt.

The sun was low on the western horizon when Frank suggested they look for a place to camp. He studied one of the guidebooks. "There's a place up the road about a hundred miles, but it sounds pretty fancy according to this. The rates are high," he announced.

Biff said, "I'd like to camp out in the open—a spot like that orchard up on the next hill."

Chet, who was driving, slowed down and glanced at the extensive orchard which swept up over the brow of the hill and down the other side.

There were no houses in sight. A small dirt lane led from the road through a broken fence into the symmetrical stand of apple trees.

"Let's spend the night here," Frank said

As Chet pulled over to the shoulder of the highway, a car passed them, then slowed and stopped.

The man in the car appeared to be studying a map, then continued on. Chet drove up the lane and pulled their camper to a fairly level spot among the trees. Eagerly the boys jumped out of the car, and in ten minutes time the trailer tent was unhitched and set in place.

"Chet, you're the great chef!" Joe remarked. "Get busy in the galley."

"Right," Biff said. "I'm hungry."

"Chow will be ready in half an hour," Chet declared with a grand gesture.

Biff went off with Sherlock, while Frank and Joe stretched out on the bunks until suppertime.

Soon the aroma of minute steaks filled the air and Chet called out, "Chow's ready." Meat and vegetables were the main course; fruit for dessert. The boys relished every mouthful. As soon as darkness fell they unzipped their sleeping bags and crawled into their bunks.

Sherlock walked round and round, seeking out a comfortable spot. He finally settled down at the foot of Chet's sleeping bag.

All four boys dozed off quickly and slept soundly until the middle of the night when a mysterious thumping on the roof awakened them. Joe whispered, "Frank, do you hear that?"

The wind had risen and whistled through the trees. Again came the *thump, thump*.

Sherlock began to whimper, and Biff tried to quiet him.

Suddenly Chet let out a cry of terror!

CHAPTER IV

Four Flats

CHET's bloodcurdling scream caused his friends to scramble out of their bunks. They fumbled for flashlights, and soon three bright beams illuminated Chet Morton. He was blinking sheepishly.

His heart still pounding, Joe asked, "Why—why did you scream, Chet?"

"I heard the knocking and it woke me up."

"We all heard it," Frank said. "Is that what made you yell?"

"Naw. Sherlock's what made me holler." Chet said that when he had reached for his flashlight, he had put his hand into the hound's mouth!

"It scared me," Chet went on. "That warm, wet tongue. Ugh! I guess Sherlock sleeps with his mouth open."

"Remind me to have his adenoids removed," Biff said with a chuckle.

"Listen, fellows," Frank put in. "How come the knocking?"

"Maybe some ghosts are conducting a séance," Biff joked.

"It isn't funny," Chet said.

Frank suggested they get out and take a look around. By now the wind had decreased, but the apple-tree branches moved slightly in the breeze.

The beams of their flashlights revealed a low-hanging limb over the camper. A cluster of green apples swayed back and forth, barely brushing against the top.

"There's the answer," Biff said. "In the high wind the apples knocked on our roof!"

"And scared all of us," Frank said. "Boy, are we ever brave!"

Before they climbed into their bunks again, Chet tied the dog to the refrigerator door. In the morning he found the door open and Sherlock poking around some well-wrapped meat. Chet scornfully ordered the hound outside and told Biff his dog would have to sleep under the stars hereafter.

"The chef's got some rights too!" Chet grumbled.

"Okay," Biff said, stretching. "Quit talking and start producing."

After he had splashed himself with cold water, Chet busied himself at the stove, while Frank, Joe, and Biff went to get some heavy sweaters from the car, which was parked about fifty feet away in a clearing.

Approaching it, Joe dashed suddenly forward. "Of all the rotten tricks!"

Frank hastened to his side. "What's the matter?"

"The tires! All four of them—flat!"

"Can't be," Biff said. "Maybe it's just the tall grass that gives it that appearance."

Closer examination disproved Biff's wishful thinking. Air had been let out of all four tires. Worse than that, someone had removed the valve cores!

"Now we're in real trouble," Frank said.

"We've got a foot pump, haven't we?" asked Biff.

"Sure, but we don't have any spare cores," Joe replied.

"Who could have done it?" Frank turned to scan the orchard as far up the hill as he could see.

Their speculation was interrupted by Chet calling, "Come and get it! Ham and eggs on the menu this morning!"

When Chet heard the bad news about the flat tires he almost dropped the skillet. "Listen," he said as he served the others, "why don't we ride down to the shore for a nice quiet holiday instead of going west?"

"Um, good eggs," Frank said, ignoring Chet's comment.

"Look, I've got part of a shell here," Biff complained with a wink.

"No extra charge," Chet said cheerfully. "If you don't like it, save it for Sherlock."

"Yeah, what about him?" Biff asked. "Has he had—?"

"I gave that hound chow first thing," Chet replied.

"Good man," Biff said. "Do we get seconds?"

"Sure."

Chet cracked two white shells and neatly dropped the eggs into the skillet.

When they finished breakfast Frank said he would have to hitchhike into the next town to buy valve cores. As he stepped out of the trailer, a short, heavy-set man wearing dungarees and a blue denim shirt strode down the hill with a look of determination on his face.

"Oh, oh. More trouble," Frank called to the others.

The three boys came outside to see what was going on. The stranger was about forty, sunburned, and with bulging biceps that bespoke days of hard manual labor.

"Good morning," Frank said pleasantly.

"What's good about it?" said the man tartly. "I can have you all arrested and I've a good mind to do it!" He introduced himself as the owner of the orchard and went on, "You kids think you can drive in here and squat on private property?"

The boys felt embarrassed, realizing that they had done the wrong thing. Frank tried to appease the farmer.

"We—we didn't see any houses around," Frank explained.

"Then you didn't look hard enough," the farmer said. He turned halfway around and pointed to the top of the ridge. "My place is right over there."

"Well, gee, we were hungry and tired," Biff put in. "All we wanted was to eat some chow and hit the sack."

"You should have asked permission to camp here," the farmer insisted.

"Don't you think you've punished us enough?" said Joe, a little more vehemently than he had intended.

"What do you mean by that?"

"All our tires are flat."

"Are you accusing me?" The farmer's jaw thrust forward, and he took a step closer.

"Oh no offense meant," Joe said. "That is if you didn't do it."

The farmer half-smiled in spite of himself. "If I wanted to punish you, I'd give you a boot in the britches."

The expression made the boys laugh. Their humor was infectious and the man joined in with a loud guffaw.

"Honest," Frank said, leading the way to the

Hardys' car. "Someone came in here last night and deflated us."

"And took the valve cores, too," Joe added. "We're really stuck."

The farmer pursed his lips and shook his head. "Too bad. But I think I can help you."

"Have you got some spares?" Frank asked quickly.

"Yep. Up in the barn. Come along, young fellow, and I'll give them to you."

Frank apologized again.

"Forget it," the farmer said. "You told me once, that's enough."

Frank had trouble keeping up with the man, whose sturdy legs were used to climbing the hill. Tagging a few feet behind, he finally came to the ridge and saw a snug farmhouse sheltered just below the brow of the slope. A barn stood nearby, with baskets stacked along the side. A mud-splattered half-ton pickup was in the driveway.

While Frank waited, the farmer went into the barn and returned with a flat, thin packet containing four valve cores.

"Let me pay you," Frank said, reaching into his pocket.

"No need. And if you want a place to camp on your way back from wherever you're going, just toot your horn a couple of times to let me know."

Frank thanked the man, then trotted over the hill. Going down the other side, he saw Biff circling the orchard with Sherlock straining at the leash. Chet and Joe followed close behind them.

When Frank caught up with the group, he asked, "What's up?"

"I had a hunch," Joe replied. "Gave Sherlock a smell of the inner sole from Whip Lasher's shoe."

"And old Sherlock picked up the trail," Biff added, restraining the hound.

Frank declared, "So that's who let the air out of our tires!"

"Didn't Collig say he was a practical joker?" Chet said. Then he shuddered. "Hey! Think what might have happened. That goon could have murdered us all in our sleep!"

Frank agreed they should be extra-cautious. The bloodhound led them closer and closer to the highway. However, when they reached the edge of the road, Sherlock lost the scent.

Suddenly Joe remembered something. "I'll bet he was the guy who stopped ahead of us when we drove in here."

"You could be right," Frank admitted.

"Sure. He waited to play his dirty trick until we were asleep."

The valve cores were replaced quickly. Using a foot pump, the boys labored hard to inflate the tires. Luckily the side walls had not separated from the rims and the boys completed the task successfully.

Leg-weary from the pumping, they folded up their camper and the caravan was on its way again. That night and the following one were spent in small trailer camps, where the fees were modest and the facilities good. They were now approaching the area where many of the Magnacard swindles had taken place.

The Hardys consulted the list of dealers who had been victimized, and stopped in stores in three different towns. There they learned that at least two other men besides Whip Lasher had purchased goods, most of it sporting equipment. They were both described as shorter than average, stout, and dark-haired.

One merchant, in particular, was furious. "Those polecats got a beautiful cabin cruiser from me," he said.

"That would be sort of hard to hide, wouldn't it?" asked Joe.

"Well, it was several days before I realized I had been swindled," the man replied. "By that time they could have been thousands of miles away from here."

"I don't think it would be easy to sell a high-priced boat like that," Frank said.

The man shrugged. "I suppose if they can't sell it they'll use it themselves."

Then he cocked his head. "You say you're after the swindlers?"

"Right," Joe replied.

"Well, I'd advise you to keep your eyes open in all camping spots."

"That's what we intend to do," Frank said.

After jotting down the cruiser's description and engine number, the boys set off on the highway again. Toward late afternoon, Joe studied the map and picked out a large trailer park fifty miles ahead.

"I'm all for stopping there," Chet said. "It's getting late."

When they pulled into the camp, the boys were surprised to see how large it was. In one section trailers were parked close together, and the vacationers sat on folding chairs, chatting with their neighbors. Some of the house trailers had plaques on the doors, with the names and addresses of their owners.

Joe drove to a secluded spot, where they quickly set up the camper. As they finished their evening meal, a loudspeaker boomed out the announcement there would be a talent show that evening.

"Come one, come all and enjoy the fun," the announcer said. "We'll meet at nine o'clock at the campfire."

"How about it, Joe?" Frank asked. "Want to show them a little Bayport talent with that guitar of yours?"

"Sure," Joe replied. "If Biff brings his mouth organ."

"Oh, come on," Biff said. "Don't you think a big guy like me would look funny playing a little bitty harmonica?"

Frank noticed the pout on Chet's face. "Now don't feel left out, Chet," he said. "Maybe you could do a hula dance. Did you bring your grass skirt?"

"Lay off, will you!" Chet retorted. "I got another surprise for you."

"What's that?" Joe asked brightly.

Somewhat embarrassed, Chet admitted that he had been practicing on a jew's-harp.

"Hey, that's great!" said Joe. "Then all three of us will do our thing!"

"Sure," Frank added. "The Bayport Symphony. I hope they have a talent scout from Hollywood here tonight."

The boys laughed, looking forward to an evening of fun. Shortly after dark the park manager trucked a load of logs to a pit in the center of the grounds. A huge bonfire was started and its flames lighted up the night.

After a crowd had gathered around, the master of ceremonies called for volunteers to entertain. One boy stepped forward with a trumpet. After a good jazz rendition, he was followed by a solo drummer.

"Not bad," Frank said. Then he introduced the Bayport Symphony. But before the boys could plunge into the folk tunes they had planned, the stillness of the evening was broken by the staccato sound of a motorcycle.

A small trail bike weaved around the edge of the crowd. The rider, a young fellow with flying blond hair, grinned devilishly at the onlookers.

The emcee ordered him away and the bike turned back. When the *put-put* of the motor faded out, Joe, Biff, and Chet launched into their act. The crowd clapped and howled with laughter as Chet did a soft-shoe while playing the jew's-harp.

Then suddenly the trail bike chattered again like a machine gun.

"That guy must be nuts," Biff declared as the driver whizzed past where they were standing.

Joe jumped out of the way, lost his balance, and dropped his guitar. Biff shook his fist at the cyclist, who turned around and headed for them again.

Nimbly the boys jumped aside, but the rider was not aiming at them. He took a leap at the guitar.

Crunch! It was cut to pieces by the trail bike!

CHAPTER V

A Strange Hiding Place

WHEN the trail bike smashed Joe's guitar, cries of dismay came from the onlookers. Joe sprinted after the rider, but his flying legs were no match for the motorbike. It arrowed out of the camp gate and disappeared down the road.

When Joe trotted back, Frank was gingerly picking up the pieces. He turned to his brother. "I'm afraid this is totaled."

Joe seethed with anger at the senseless act of destruction.

Chet said, "Some nerve that creep's got! He's driving around on the main road without lights or even a vehicle registration. Someone'll catch up with him sooner or later!"

"That someone's going to be me!" Joe vowed. He took the remains of his instrument and tossed them into a trash can.

The Hardys wondered whether the youth had a trailer in the area, and began to query the people who had gathered around to offer consolations to the Bayport Symphony. All were incensed over the vicious incident.

Light from the big bonfire flickered across their concerned faces as they gave Frank and Joe some bits and pieces of information. Several campers had seen the blond youth before. One of them, a man from Texas, had warned him to use the unlicensed cycle only on the mountain trails.

"But of course he paid no attention to me," the man said.

A young woman pushed her way through the crowd and told Joe, "If you're looking for that mean boy I may know where he's staying."

"You do?" Joe said in surprise. "Where?"

The woman said that the day before the same trail bike had zipped past her on the highway, then turned onto a dirt road. "I saw it pull up to a camp," she said. "It's two and a half miles from here, off to the right."

Joe thanked her and decided to visit the place the next morning.

That night Sherlock was tied up outside and the night passed quietly.

"What are you going to tell that hoodlum when you see him?" Chet asked as he prepared breakfast.

"Nothing," Joe replied. "I'm going to punch him in the nose."

"That is if you find him," Biff said. "Suppose he's left already?"

"Come on, Chet. Hurry up," Joe said. "We can't wait all day for the sausages."

Half an hour later they were ready to go. Frank drove out of the area and onto the highway. Exactly two and a half miles down the road Frank slowed, and the boys peered into the heavy growth of trees and brush on the right side.

"Look, I see it!" Joe called out. "Turn here, Frank."

The lane, made by car wheels, was barely visible. Frank drove in slowly with twigs cracking under the tires. As they approached a small clearing they saw a trailer, the kind that normally sleeps two. No car was in evidence, but the trail bike was propped against a tree. Painted on the gas tank were two words: *Vampire Trail.*

The only person in sight was the blond-haired youth. He was washing tin dishes in a pan of water. When the car drew nearer, he turned around. Joe got out first, walked up to him, and said, "I'm Joe Hardy. Who are you?"

The boy pushed the hair from his eyes with the back of his hand. "Name's Juice Barden. What do you want?" He had a thin face and light-blue eyes which blinked nervously. Joe judged him to be about eighteen years old.

"Look, you broke my guitar last night," Joe said.

"So?"

"So it's no joke. You're going to pay for it!"

"Now there's a real joke," Juice said arrogantly. "You didn't get out of the way fast enough."

"You've got no right to buzz a trail bike around a crowd of people!"

"La-de-da," replied Juice. He reached down, picked up a half-empty bottle of orange soda, and took a swig.

Infuriated, Joe cocked his right arm and was about to let fly with a punch when Biff grabbed him. "Don't hit Junior, he's no match for you," Biff said. "We'll just wait to see his father and tell him what a bad boy he has."

Juice sneered, "You think you're great because there are four of you."

Chet, meanwhile, was strolling around the campsite. From nails driven into the trees hung a few pieces of drying laundry and a blackened skillet. Chet spied a guitar dangling on a leather thong.

"Hey, Joe, look at this!" he called out. "You want a guitar? Here's one!" Chet lifted the instrument off the nail and walked over to Joe.

Juice took a step forward but thought better of interfering. "You can't take that!" he declared.

"Oh no? I'll keep it until you buy me a new one," Joe said.

Juice replied coolly, "Fingers won't like it."

"Fingers?" asked Chet. "Who's he?"

"You'll know soon enough."

The four boys shrugged and turned to leave. Joe looked back for a moment. "Okay, Barden. Tell Fingers the guitar is in good hands."

"What a crumb!" Chet muttered as they got into the car.

"I wonder who this Fingers is," said Biff.

"My guess," Joe said, "is that he's some fancy pants dumb-dumb. What's the old saying—birds of a feather flock together?"

"Is it a good guitar?" asked Biff as Frank started off.

"Fair, I'd say," Joe declared after strumming a few notes. "Mine was a lot better."

They sped westward for an hour and when Biff spelled Frank at the wheel they stopped to admire a spectacular waterfall. It gushed out from a crevice in the pine hills and churned white on rocks close to the road's edge, before boiling under the highway bridge. The boys got out and stood on the bridge to enjoy the sight, until Biff became impatient.

"Come on. We're wasting too much time," he said, and walked toward the car which was parked off the bridge on the side of the road.

As the others ambled along behind Biff, a sedan pulling a small trailer, squealed past them and drove up directly in front of the Hardys' convertible. Juice's trail bike was lashed to the rear of the sedan.

The doors opened and out jumped Juice Barden and two others. One was a youth about Juice's age, who had frizzy hair, droopy eyelids, and a sullen expression. The other was a man in his twenties, thin, agile, and as tall as Biff.

"These are the ones," Juice said to the tall man.

Frank looked at him. "I suppose you're Fingers."

"I'm Fingers, all right." The man turned to the droopy-eyed youth. "Rip, you and Juice look for my guitar."

"Oh no you don't!" said Joe. "This buddy of yours crushed mine with his trail bike!"

"Juice is no responsibility of mine," Fingers replied coldly.

"Don't be tough!" Biff spoke up and stepped forward. "You'll get your guitar when you pay Joe for his."

"Oh yeah? How much?"

"Fifty dollars," Joe replied.

"Out of sight," retorted Fingers as his two pals slowly walked to the Hardys' car.

"Touch that and I'll flatten you!" Biff thundered.

"We'll see about that!" snapped Fingers. His right hand flew to his pocket. He pulled out a knife, pressed a button, and a switchblade flashed in the sunlight. "Okay now, we'll take my guitar," he said with a menacing sneer.

Frank's mind whirled. "Better not push this too

far," he thought, "or somebody'll really get hurt."
Aloud he said, "Okay, Fingers, I guess you win
this time." He walked to the car, got the guitar,
and approached Fingers. As he did, Biff edged
closer.

"Here, take it," Frank offered.

As the man reached for the instrument, Biff
lashed out with a karate kick. The toe of his boot
caught Fingers' wrist, sending the knife flying.

Biff followed up with a chop and Fingers
landed on his back. As he struggled to his feet,
Rip jumped on Frank and wrestled him to the
ground. Juice threw a punch at Joe.

"You asked for it," Joe muttered. With a left-
hand feint and a right-hand cross to the jaw, he
sent Juice sprawling. The battle was short. Without his knife, Fingers was no match for Biff. Chet
picked up the knife and the seven stood there glar-
ing at one another.

Fingers' guitar lay broken.

"Okay," Frank said. "That evens things up.
One broken guitar a piece." He bent over to pick
up Fingers' smashed instrument and his eyes wid-
ened. Inside were some blue stones, glued to the
wood.

"What are these?" Frank asked.

Wincing, Fingers reached out for the guitar.
"None of your business," he muttered. He took
the fractured instrument, turned, and climbed
into his car. Juice and Rip followed and they

drove off. The Hardys passed them a few miles down the road.

Frank, meanwhile, had been thinking about the stones. Obviously they had been hidden for a reason. "Sapphires are blue, aren't they, Joe?" he asked.

"Sure. Don't you remember, Mother's birthstone?" Joe shook his head. "You missed a chance to get her a present, Frank!"

Shortly afterward they stopped at a rest area to have lunch, then rode on for the balance of the afternoon. It was four o'clock when they reached a sparkling lake. Its sandy beach had accommodations for a few trailers and Joe eased their camper to a shady spot close to the water.

"How about a swim, fellows?" he asked.

They were all eager to get into the cool water and soon had put on their swim trunks which they kept handy in the car.

"What'll we do with Sherlock?" Biff asked, reaching into the car's trunk for a towel.

"Tie him to the bumper," Frank advised. "We'll let him have a dip when we're finished."

The boys raced into the water, their arms and legs flying. Strong strokes carried them far out. Chet rolled over and floated on his back, spewing a plume of water into the air.

Frank chuckled. "There's good old Chet the whale."

Encouraged by this remark, Chet dived and sur-

Biff sent the knife flying

faced like a porpoise. As Joe watched him, he looked back and saw another car parked near the water's edge. Two men got out.

"Look, fellows!" Joe cried in alarm.

One of the men produced a bottle from his car, then lighted a wick at the mouth of it.

"It's a Molotov cocktail!" Frank gasped.

With swift strokes the boys churned toward shore. But they were not in time to prevent the men from hurling the bottle at the camper. It burst in a sheet of flame as the pair jumped into their car and sped off.

The bloodhound, unable to get away, strained at the leash and howled pitifully.

Biff yelled, "Sherlock's going to get burned!"

CHAPTER VI

Midnight Stakeout

REACHING shore, the boys dashed to the camper. Flames were blazing close to the terrified bloodhound.

Biff untied the dog while Frank, Joe, and Chet threw sand on the fire. Then Biff grabbed the fire extinguisher from the Hardys' car and doused the last of the flames.

The boys assessed the damage. Paint had been burned off the side of the trailer and one of the tires gave off a pungent odor. But the damage was slight.

"Thank goodness Sherlock wasn't hurt," Frank said, bending to scratch the dog's ears.

Chet said, "Somebody's really out to get us."

"And you can bet it's Fingers," Biff added.

As they dressed, Frank said, "Biff, I doubt that it was Fingers who did this."

"Why?"

"Because he would have done it himself. Neither of those men was Fingers, or his pals. It looks more like Whip Lasher's mob."

"Another one of his practical jokes?" Biff said. Frank nodded.

The boys hit the road again. Two hours later the low hills they were passing through flattened out to rolling prairie as far as the eye could see.

"Where are we going to camp tonight?" Joe asked.

"We'd better stay away from a popular trailer court," Frank said.

"Let's get a secluded place," Biff suggested.

"Right," Joe agreed. "I'll take my sleeping bag and station myself a distance away in case we should have more visitors."

As the sun began to set, Chet was at the wheel. He noticed a cleared area in a cornfield which seemed to stretch for miles. "How about this?" he asked.

Frank and Joe looked about for any sign of habitation. There was none. Chet pulled off the road close to the green stand of head-high corn. The trailer was unhitched, and the camper set up.

"Let me take the galley tonight," Joe said. "You look kind of pooped after that long drive, Chet."

"Okay," Chet said and stretched himself out on one of the bunks.

After sundown, darkness dropped like a blanket

over the warm prairie. Joe took his sleeping bag, walked toward the road, and found a nook between rows of corn.

He slept intermittently, an occasional passing car stirring him to semiwakefulness. Shortly after midnight he heard the distant noise of a motorbike. Then the bike stopped.

Joe crept out of the sleeping bag, crouched, and listened. From the side of the road someone with a covered flashlight was approaching. There was no beam, just an eerie red eye searching through the cornstalks.

Joe decided to surprise the prowler. "Who are you?" he demanded.

The challenge stopped the prowler in his tracks. A voice from the dark said, "You know who I am. You palmed some of my sapphires. Now give them back!"

Fingers again! What was he up to now?

"We didn't take any of your sapphires. Maybe you dropped them along the road," Joe said.

"Impossible."

"Perhaps Juice or Rip took them."

Fingers did not advance. It seemed obvious that the man was thinking over what Joe had said.

The young detective took advantage of the pause. "Is that why you fire-bombed us this afternoon?"

"Fire-bombed! Are you crazy?"

"Don't deny it!"

"I wouldn't try to burn anybody." Fingers sounded as if his feelings were hurt.

Just then Sherlock started to bark.

"Don't turn that mutt on me!" Fingers cried.

His light retreated to the side of the road and disappeared. A few minutes later Joe heard the whine and staccato of the bike's motor as it came to life, then the sounds gradually faded and the night was still.

"Hey, Joe! What's the matter? Any trouble?" It was Frank.

The boys gathered outside the camper and Joe told what had happened.

"So those stones were really sapphires," Frank said. "I wonder where he got them."

"Probably stole them, and now he claims we took them from him," Joe said.

"I believe the other two guys swiped them," said Chet. "They didn't strike me as being trustworthy."

"And he denied the fire-bombing?" Biff asked.

"Downright emphatic about it," Joe reported. "I think that underneath, Fingers has a soft heart!"

Biff grumbled, "You'd have to prove that to me."

"Anyhow," Frank said, "it seems that our three friends don't trust one another." He pointed out that Juice obviously had not known about the concealed gems when Chet lifted the guitar from the nail in the tree.

"I'm going to phone Dad tomorrow morning and tell him the circumstances," Frank said as they all settled down for the rest of the night.

At dawn Frank roused the others. By the time the sun had risen, breakfast was over and the camping gear stowed for the next leg of their journey.

At the first town Frank stopped to telephone Bayport. His father was away on his case. Mrs. Hardy, who usually was calm, seemed agitated. "Frank, we got a strange letter," she said.

"About what, Mother?"

"About you. Wait while I get it."

Mrs. Hardy returned a few moments later and read the message. It was addressed to Mr. and Mrs. Fenton Hardy and said:

I KNOW THAT YOUR SONS ARE ON THE
WAY WEST TO TRACK DOWN THE GREAT
WL. KEEP THEM OUT OF THE ROCKIES
OR THEY WILL NEVER GET BACK ALIVE.

"Who sent it?" Frank asked.

"I don't know. It's unsigned and was sent air-mail from Indiana," his mother replied.

"Don't worry," Frank told her. "We're capable

of taking care of ourselves. Someone has been bothering us and now I'm sure that it's Whip Lasher and his gang."

Frank decided not to mention the fire-bombing. He said that if his father called to tell him that the trail had been cold to medium. When it got hot, Joe or he would phone home again.

It was afternoon when the flat prairie gave way to a clutch of low hills on the western horizon. The boys had not seen Fingers and his pals and hoped that they had turned either north or south.

"That Terrible Trio really bugs me," Biff said.

At a curve in the road a woman stood beside a disabled car, waving a white handkerchief.

"Okay, Sir Galahad," Chet told Frank, who was driving. "Pull over and we'll give yon damsel a sample of our superb chivalry."

"She has a flat tire," Frank said. "Want to change it?" He braked slowly, stopping on the downgrade some distance ahead of the disabled car. All four got out and walked back.

The woman, attractive and in her twenties, smiled nervously as the boys approached. "Will you please help me?" she asked. "I've never changed a tire in my life."

"Yes, ma'am," Joe said. "Chet here has volunteered to do the job."

"How thoughtful," the woman replied. "Then I suppose you're a mechanic."

Chet's look of chagrin turned to one of proud

pleasure. "Sure. I can do almost anything with a car. Is your spare in the trunk?"

She nodded and handed him the key.

Chet found the jack and soon had the rear end several inches off the ground. He removed the rim and tried to replace it with the spare. It would not fit!

"Having trouble, Chet?" asked Biff.

The perspiring boy glared and the woman said, "Chet, I think you're putting it on backward."

"Oh yes. Thank you." Chet reversed the wheel and it snapped quickly into place.

"I guess the heat got to me," Chet said, screwing the lugs back on. Then he banged the hubcap in place. While he was doing this, several cars drove past. Joe was on the alert, watching for Fingers' trailer but it did not come by.

As Chet replaced the tools, the woman suddenly put a hand to her mouth and cried, "My goodness, isn't that your car?"

All heads whipped to the spot where they had parked. Their car and the camper were moving slowly down the incline.

"I don't believe it!" Frank shouted. "I'm sure I set the brakes!"

He dashed ahead of the others as the car picked up speed. It was impossible to overtake it! All at once he noticed the young woman driving alongside him.

"I'll help you!" she called out.

Frank flung his arm into the open right-hand window and hung on. The woman put on speed and soon her car and the Hardys' were side by side.

"Closer! Can you come closer?" Frank shouted.

The two vehicles were now hardly more than a couple of feet apart and Frank saw Sherlock looking forlornly out the back window.

Frank made a lunge, releasing his hold on the woman's car and clutching at the steering wheel of his own. A pain shot up along his arm. His fingers nearly lost their grip but he held on. The car was heading off the side of the road toward a deep gully. Frank struggled desperately to control it!

CHAPTER VII

Charred Evidence

FRANK gripped the door and with a mighty wrench pulled his shoulders through the window opening. Then he wriggled onto the seat, jammed on the brakes, cut the motor, and twisted the wheel. The car lurched to a halt on the lip of the embankment.

"The trailer!" Frank thought. He hardly dared to look behind. The camper dangled over the gully! The slightest motion might send it and the car crashing down.

Joe, Chet, and Biff raced to assist Frank. While they grabbed the car so it would not teeter, Frank opened the door and slid out.

Sherlock jumped into the front seat and bounded out into Biff's arms.

"Some camping trip!" Chet muttered. "We spend half of our time rescuing Sherlock!"

Joe said, "This is either more of Fingers' work, or Whip Lasher's!"

"We didn't see Fingers' trailer go by," Chet remarked.

"Well, if it was Fingers, he and his pals must be somewhere near here," Frank said. "We'll search for them after we get our camper back on the road."

As he spoke, a large transcontinental truck moved cautiously down the grade and Joe hailed it. "Can you pull us back on the highway?" he asked.

The truckers said they would be glad to. From their gear locker they pulled out a long chain, which they attached to the front of the Hardys' car. Then carefully—a few inches at a time—the large vehicle eased the car and the trailer up over the edge and back onto the shoulder of the road.

"Thanks a lot!" Frank said.

The truckers replied with a salute and left.

"They're great guys in an emergency," Biff declared.

Frank turned around and headed back. A couple of miles along the road they saw a rest area they had not noticed before. Two small trailers were parked next to picnic tables, where four people sat, eating and chatting.

"Hi, there," Frank said as he approached the two middle-aged couples.

"Hello, boys," one of the women said. "If you're hungry, sit right down and join us."

"No, thank you," Frank replied. "We were just

looking for a small trailer. We thought it might have been parked here."

"The one with the Vampire Trail motorbike?"

"That's right."

"They left a while ago," her husband added. "After they cooked some grub over a fire." He pointed to a stone pit about twenty-five feet away.

"Which way were they headed?" asked Biff.

"West," the other man said.

"Funny," mused Chet, "we didn't see them on the road."

"That's because they decided to take a shortcut by a back road. Look, it's here on the map."

He handed Frank a road map and traced the line of a secondary road. "It might be a little rough," he added, "but it avoids the traffic on the highway."

Frank thanked him and said in a low voice to Joe, "I've got it figured. One of them drove past in their car, released our brake, turned around and came back here. Then they high-tailed off through the hinterland so we wouldn't see them!"

Chet, meanwhile, had wandered off to the stone pit. At the edge of the stones lay the charred remains of a camping magazine.

"Oh, Frank! Here's something that might interest you."

He picked up the magazine and gave it to Frank. In it were the usual stories about good

camping sites, a rundown on new models of motor-
bikes, and a section on house trailers.

Frank turned another page. "Look at this, Joe,"
he said. A short article was titled "Sapphire
Trek." The dateline had been burned off, but
most of the text was intact. It told of illegal mining of precious stones in the Rockies. The following page had been torn out.

Frank and Joe looked at each other. Both were
asking themselves the same questions. Had the
sapphires in the guitar been mined illegally? Did
Fingers and his gang have anything to do with
such an operation?

The Hardys talked it over and decided there
must be some connection. They discussed their
theory with Chet and Biff.

"If they tore out a page, it proves they were interested in something to do with the mine," Biff
agreed.

Chet said, "So now we have two mysteries.
Which one are we going to concentrate on,
Frank?"

The Hardys were determined to follow their
original case. Scant as clues had been, they had
a hunch that Whip Lasher was not only following
them for the purpose of harassment, but also was
heading for a hideout in the Rockies.

Frank tossed the magazine into a trash can. The
boys said good-by to the couples, and continued

on their way. Biff was driving, with Joe next to him. Biff said, "I think the Terrible Trio will keep out of our sight from now on."

"Right," Joe said. "They'll know we suspect them of releasing the brake."

In the back seat Chet hooked his thumbs into his belt and heaved a sigh of relief. "If we never see them again, it'll be too soon."

Frank studied the map as they went over mountainous terrain. "Denver is not far away," he said. "A couple of hundred miles or so."

The sun hung red on the horizon and Biff flipped the driver's visor down to cut the glare. Up ahead he could see a car hauling a shiny white cabin cruiser on a boat trailer.

"Are you thinking what I'm thinking?" asked Joe.

Biff nodded and reduced his speed to follow behind the boat. The boys studied it in detail, comparing it with the one bought with the counterfeit credit card. It fitted the description perfectly.

"But let's not jump to conclusions," Frank warned Joe.

"We could stop him right away!" Joe said.

"Negative. If we make a citizen's arrest and we're wrong—"

"Frank's right," Biff put in. "If this fellow is going to camp overnight, how about buddying up?"

"Great idea," Chet said. "Besides, I'm getting hungry."

A half mile farther on a huge sign announced that a flood control and hydroelectric power reservoir lay ten miles ahead. Campers were welcome.

Frank consulted the map. "Wow! This place is twenty miles long and about five miles wide!"

"I'll bet that's where our friend's going," Biff said.

His guess proved correct. The next fork in the road had a sign: *Turn left to Badland Reservoir. State boating laws in effect.*

Frank dropped to a discreet distance behind the boat trailer. It headed directly to the shore of the lake and parked in the camping area.

The Hardys pulled up alongside and set up their camper. Frank had warned the others not to pay any attention to their neighbor but to busy themselves around their own trailer.

The plan worked well. Biff unlimbered his fishing rod and began casting it into the reservoir. Joe tinkered under the hood of the car, checking the oil, while Frank and Chet prepared supper. Finally the door of the other car opened. A man got out and warily watched the boys. He was in his middle thirties, stout, with receding black hair, a large nose, and small eyes. His shelving chin added to the general appearance of a sleek beaver.

He approached the steps of the camper,

knocked, and when Frank came out, introduced himself as Edward K. Mungo.

"Pretty efficient layout you boys have here," he said.

"We like it," Frank replied.

"What's your name?" the man asked.

"I'm Frank. The chef is Chet. The guy fishing is Biff. And the other one is Joe."

Chet, meanwhile, continued his stint at the stove, cutting up three large onions into a skillet with melted butter.

Frank said, "Mr. Mungo likes the smell of our chow. What do you say we invite him to dinner?"

Chet nodded and the man said, "That's very friendly of you. Thank you. I accept with pleasure."

When the meal was over, Mungo said, "It's a lucky thing you fellows parked near me. How would you like to help me launch my cruiser?"

"Glad to," Frank said.

The hitch was uncoupled and the boys trundled the cruiser into the reservoir. Mungo started the motor, waved, and set out with a throaty purr of the engine.

Darkness was falling but not fast enough to conceal another boat coming up to meet the cruiser. Both craft stopped, with motors idling.

"I'd like to take a look at what's going on out there," Frank said.

"We've got our foldboat," Biff remarked. "Let's put it together."

The two-seater collapsible boat was pulled out of the trunk of their car and quickly inflated. Frank and Joe got in and paddled silently across the dark waters.

They came as close as they dared to the two boats. The sounds of voices drifted over the lake, but the conversation was not clear enough to be understandable. Suddenly the conversation ceased. A powerful flashlight illuminated the area. Frank and Joe ducked and began to paddle back toward land. When they reached the shore, Biff and Chet were waiting.

"Quick, put the boat away," Frank said.

He and Joe stood on the shore while the others deflated the boat and stowed it. They waited a long time but the cruiser did not reappear.

"He'll have to come back some time," Frank said. "Well, let's hit the sack. We can check that guy out in the morning."

The four slept soundly. At daybreak they rose, dressed, and stepped out onto the dewy grass to see whether the boat had returned.

"He came back all right," Chet said, pointing to a cruiser drifting at anchor a few feet from shore. "Mungo's probably sleeping aboard."

"Why not blow the whistle on him right now, Frank?" Biff asked.

"Not so fast," Frank replied. "Take a look at that boat again."

The boys peered through the mist rising over the reservoir. Biff exclaimed, "It's not the same one!"

"Correct," Frank stated. "Mungo pulled a switch during the night!"

CHAPTER VIII

The Missing Cruiser

THEIR evidence against the Magnacard swindlers had vanished! The boat lying at anchor in the still waters of the reservoir was not the one they had trailed along the highway.

"What'll we do now?" Chet asked.

"Play it cool," Frank replied. "Mungo's probably sleeping out there. If we act suspiciously, he might give us the slip."

It was decided that he and Joe would take the rubber boat and scout the reservoir. If they had any important news for Chet and Biff, who were to keep an eye on Mungo, they would report it over their two-way radio.

Just then the boat they were watching rocked a little, sending a small ripple over the quiet surface.

"Let's duck," Joe suggested. "Mungo's probably getting up."

Frank carried the foam boat some distance down the shore, while Joe lugged the small motor. When they were safely out of Mungo's earshot, they unlimbered the boat, attached the motor, and cruised along the shore, keeping a sharp lookout for the white craft.

The sun grew hot, dispelling the mist over the reservoir. Along the shore were more campers than the boys had imagined. Some were in trailers, while others emerged from bright striped tents and waded into the water for a morning swim.

Boats began to move across the lake. Some were small; others were as large as the white cruiser.

"We'll be all day at this job," Frank said, scanning the long shoreline. It stretched for miles ahead before curving around toward the low hills on the other side of the lake.

The Hardys pulled ashore several times to ask campers if they had seen the white cabin cruiser but no one had. At noon they approached land to quiz a number of boys and girls who were their own age. All ran down to the water's edge to greet Frank and Joe as they beached their boat.

"Hi," Frank said, stepping out. He introduced himself and his brother.

The young people proved to be high school students from Kansas City, who had driven west on vacation. Their chaperons, Mr. and Mrs. Rickle, gave the Hardys a warm welcome.

Joe spoke up. "Mrs. Rickle, do you mind answering some questions?"

"Not at all," the woman replied.

One of the girls who had crowded around giggled. "Is this a Gallup poll or something?" she asked.

Joe grinned. "Nothing like that," he replied. "We're looking for a cruiser."

"What kind of cruiser?" Mr. Rickle inquired.

After Frank described it, Mr. Rickle remarked, "Pretty classy job." He turned to the campers. "Have any of you seen one like it in this area?"

The group had been paddling around the reservoir for three days, but no one had seen a boat that fitted the Hardys' description.

"Did you lose it?" Mrs. Rickle asked half-jokingly.

"Someone else did," Frank said.

"It would be pretty hard to lose a thing like that," one of the girls remarked. She had long flaxen hair and a quizzical smile.

"All right," Joe said with an embarrassed grin. "It was stolen. We're on the trail of it."

"Are you sure it's on this lake?" the girl went on.

"Don't be so nosy, Barbie," the woman said.

"I'm sorry, Mom."

"You don't have to be sorry," Frank said. "We're the curious type ourselves."

The girl laughed and Frank said, "Well, thanks a lot. We'd better be moving along."

Mr. Rickle glanced at his watch, then to a barbecue pit in front of one of the tents, where hot dogs were roasting on a grill.

"You can't go without food," he said.

"Well, we really—" Frank protested.

"Come to think of it," Joe interrupted, looking at Barbie, "I'm hungry."

"That settles it." Mr. Rickle grinned. "Come and join us. If you don't mind sitting on the ground, that is. We're not fancy."

The campers laughed and joked, their appetites whetted by the aroma of sizzling frankfurters. Barbie popped a chef's hat on her head, speared the hot dogs with a long fork, laid them deftly on the rolls and sang out, "Come and get 'em while they're hot!"

The Hardys ate two apiece, thanked their hosts, and said good-by.

"But you can't go without some cake," Barbie shrieked.

"Honestly," Frank said, "I'm stuffed."

The girl, however, would not take no for an answer. She wrapped two huge pieces of chocolate layer cake in aluminum foil, tucked them into a small paper bag, and handed it to Joe.

"Thanks," Joe said. "You've been awfully kind to us."

The Rickles waved as the rubber boat putted away.

Another dozen stops were made along the shore to question campers. Some had vague recollections of having seen the white cruiser. But nothing definite turned up. By now they were on the far side of the reservoir and the sun was low. A strong wind churned the water to whitecaps.

"We'd better get back," said Joe, who was at the tiller. He turned the bow of the boat into the waves and started across the wide expanse of water, but made little progress against the wind.

"This outboard isn't strong enough," Frank said. "We're getting nowhere fast."

Joe turned about and skirted the shore, hoping the wind would die down. Instead, it increased in intensity.

"Looks as if we're stuck for the night," Frank said.

They decided to find a sheltered place where they might put up. Joe steered closer to the shore, scanning the hills which sloped directly to the water without any beach whatever.

"Hey, look up ahead," Frank said, pointing.

There was a small cave at water level. Obviously the action of the waves had eroded soil and rocks in the embankment.

"We could duck in there for protection," Joe said.

By bending their heads low, the rubber boat

slid into the small pocket cave. The roof was high enough so they could sit upright.

"Good luck so far," Frank said.

They waited for the wind to subside. After about an hour, the lake gradually grew calmer.

"What about Chet and Biff?" Joe asked. "They're probably wondering where we are."

"I'll try to raise them on the radio," Frank replied.

Their friends had been instructed to leave the waveband open in case of an emergency. Frank flicked on his set and called. Biff answered. "What are you doing? Where are you? When are you coming back?"

Frank told him about their predicament, then said, "What's going on over there? Where's Chet?"

"He's keeping an eye on Mungo."

"Then he hasn't left yet?"

"No." Biff added that Mungo had asked some pointed questions during the day about the Hardys' boat trip.

"Did he see us leaving?" asked Frank.

"Right," Biff said. "He had his binoculars trained on you all the time. Chet and I spied him just as you shoved off."

"Then he's not quite so friendly as he was?"

"You can say that again. And he hasn't taken very kindly to Sherlock. He eyes him suspiciously."

"Stick with it," Frank said. "If Mungo leaves,

let us know right away. See you in the morning."

Frank had just signed off when Joe said, "Look out there!"

The running lights of a boat gleamed in the dusk. They pushed their boat close to the cave opening and strained their eyes to peer into the gloom. A white craft moved past, nearing the shore at low speed.

"That's the cruiser!" Joe hissed.

Quickly the boys guided their boat out of the cave, started the outboard, and began to trail the craft. They followed it stealthily.

The cruiser approached a cluster of lights on the shore ahead.

"Looks like a marina," Frank whispered. "Steer as close as you can, Joe."

The cruiser sounded its horn in three short blasts and several men appeared quickly at the water's edge.

Joe stopped the outboard, then paddled nearer to the marina. Flashlights bobbed. The boys eased themselves out of the rubber boat, tied it up, and crept along the shore. Now they could hear the conversation.

"The boss'll like this deal," a man said. "I sold it to a sucker down the pond a piece. To be delivered in the morning."

"Good work, good work," another man praised. "Did you sell it as is?"

"No. He wants a blue model."

"So it needs a paint job."

"Right. Otherwise it's clean. All identification has been removed."

Soon there came the gentle hiss of paint being sprayed on the cruiser.

Frank and Joe did not dare to whisper. If they were heard, they would be easy prey to the thieves.

Hours passed. Finally the first man spoke again. "Okay, the job's done. Radio E. K. and tell him to scram, if he hasn't gone already."

Mungo's initials!

Frank and Joe backed up quietly. When they were certain they were out of earshot, Frank said, "We'll call Chet and Biff to detain Mungo."

They crept back to the boat, reached for the radio, and switched it on. "Chet. Biff. This is Joe calling."

A sleepy voice replied. "Chet here. What's up?"

"Grab Mungo and don't let him get away!"

Suddenly lights shone not twenty feet from where they crouched. An angry voice boomed out, "We're being spied on!"

Cries went up from the gang near the cruiser. Shouting and cursing, the men raced along the shore, their flashlights bobbing.

The man closest to the Hardys made a lunge for them as they slipped into their boat. Would they get away?

CHAPTER IX

Sanctuary

In feverish haste Frank and Joe shoved off from the shore. Their pursuer made one last desperate lunge with a knife, half falling into the water as the tip of the blade dug into the rubber boat!

Joe started the outboard, giving it full power. Their escape was painfully slow. They felt the cold water slowly seeping through the rent in the rubberized fabric.

Their pursuer pulled himself out of the water and raced back to his confederates. Joe saw them launch a small motorboat into the reservoir. It started with a roar.

"Frank, I don't think we can make it!" Joe said, keeping their little craft close to shore and seeking the sanctuary of the small cave.

"It must be up ahead," Frank said anxiously.

Joe brought the boat so close to shore that they could nearly touch the rocks.

The speedboat, meanwhile, whined angrily as it cut across toward them.

Finally Frank spotted the cave. "Joe, there it is! Right up ahead!"

They ducked and eased into the safety of the cave. Seconds later the motorboat flashed past and droned out of earshot.

"Whew!" Frank felt the side of the boat until his fingers found the cut. "Joe, reach in for the first-aid kit, will you?"

"What for?"

"Adhesive. I think I can fix the tear with it." Frank patched the tape firmly over the rip. "Now it'll hold tight. But we've got to get the water out of here."

Joe took off his sweat shirt and sopped up the water in the bottom of the boat. After wringing out the shirt a number of times, the floor was fairly dry.

As the boys sat waiting for their pursuers to return, Frank said, "Boy, am I hungry!"

"Hey!" Joe exclaimed. "The chocolate cake!"

He pulled out a package from under his seat. The cake was slightly damp, but tasted delicious to the two hungry boys.

"Bless that Barbie," Frank said, after swallowing the last crumb.

Again they heard the motorboat. It crisscrossed the water not far from shore, then headed for the marina.

"I guess they think we sank," Joe said.

Frank nodded. "Let's start now," he said. "Keep that motor at low speed until we're far out."

The sky was velvety blue and the wind had abated completely. Stars could be seen briefly above the cover of cirrus clouds.

With a burping cough the outboard came to life and propelled the craft out into the lake. It crept along for ten minutes until Joe gave it more power. He aimed straight for the opposite shore. An hour later they reached the other side, slightly north of where their car was parked.

"Easy now, Joe," Frank warned as they edged along the shore. "We don't want to bang into Mungo's boat!"

They came to the spot where the suspect's car had stood. It was gone, and so was his boat!

"Frank!" Joe exclaimed after he had scanned the area. "Our car's not here, either!" Only the camper remained, dimly silhouetted against the eastern sky.

"Chet and Biff might have parked it somewhere else. Come on."

The boys climbed out of the boat. They pulled it ashore, then ran to the trailer. Frank opened the door and they walked inside. They played their flashlights about. The place was empty, except for Sherlock. He lay on the floor in a deep slumber.

"Frank, something happened here," Joe said. "That hound's not sleeping, he's unconscious!"

"And where are Biff and Chet?" Frank wondered. "Maybe they're in trouble!"

Joe ran back to the boat and got the radio. They tried to raise their friends over the air, but had no success.

"What now?" Joe asked.

"Let's follow the tracks."

Frank shone his light on the ground and picked up the tire marks of their car. But instead of heading toward the highway, the trail circled to the left.

"See here, Frank," Joe said. "There's only one set of tracks. Where'd Mungo go?"

Before they had a chance to ponder this, their car loomed up ahead. The Hardys ran to it and shone their lights inside. Chet and Biff were in the back seat, tied up!

Frank and Joe swung the doors open and dragged their friends out. Chet was unconscious, but Biff began to mutter. The boys chafed their hands and massaged their necks, until Biff could talk coherently and Chet revived.

"What happened?" Frank asked.

Biff explained that Mungo had driven off to get some ice cream. "We thought he was returning the favor. for having eaten chow with us," Biff said.

"The stuff tasted kind of funny," Chet put in.

"I didn't like it either." Biff made a face. "And Mungo wouldn't have any at all. So Sherlock ate most of it."

The pair related that they had suddenly become groggy. Unable to defend themselves, Mungo had tied them up, put them into the car, and parked them in the woods.

"Did you see where he went?" asked Joe.

"No. How's Sherlock?" Biff said.

"In the camper, unconscious. That's how we knew something was wrong. Well, let's get back."

Frank drove the car to their campsite. Biff ran into the trailer and bent over Sherlock, then he shook his head sadly. "Poor dog's awfully sick," he said, stroking the animal's back. "We'll have to locate a vet."

The boys lifted the dog gently and carried him to the car. The tent was folded away in the trailer and they set off.

By the time they arrived in the nearest town, the sun was up. They asked a passer-by where they could find a veterinarian and were directed to Dr. Cameron's Animal Hospital.

"He lives on the second floor," the man said. "Just ring the bell."

Biff carried the dog to the door and the Hardys followed with Chet. Frank said, "We should really do some sleuthing about that ice cream. You stay here till we get back, Biff."

"Okay," Biff said and rang the doorbell.

The three boys walked around town until they came to a large ice-cream stand. The man who was cleaning up the place turned out to be the pro-

Chet and Biff were tied up!

prietor. Frank asked whether he had sold any ice cream the previous day to a man resembling Mungo.

"Oh yes, I remember him," the man replied. "He bought a half-gallon brick—strawberry and chocolate with peach ripple in the middle."

"You've got a good memory," Joe said, pleased with their quick success.

"I couldn't forget that guy," the man replied. "He walked down the end of the counter, split the brick in the middle, and poured something on it."

"Didn't you think that was strange?" Frank asked.

"Sure. Why didn't he wait till he got home before he cut it up and poured syrup over it? But there are all kinds of weird people."

"It wasn't syrup, it was poison!" Joe declared hotly.

The proprietor blanched. "Are you sure? Did anybody get sick?"

"Not real bad," Frank said. "Only our dog."

The man looked distressed. "I'm awfully sorry," he said. He reached into the freezer and pulled out another half-gallon brick. "Maybe you'd like to have this to make up for it," he said.

"No thanks," Frank said. "It wasn't your fault."

Their next stop was at police headquarters. The boys told the deputy chief in charge about the poisoned ice cream and the stolen cruiser, and he promised to put out an all-points bulletin for Mungo and his pals at the marina.

When Frank, Joe, and Chet returned to the animal hospital, Biff was sitting outside on the steps holding his head in his hands.

"He really loves that dog," Chet said as they walked up to him.

"Hi, Biff," Frank called out. "How's old Sherlock?"

Biff replied with a long face, "Not good. I don't think he'll make it!"

CHAPTER X

Buckskin Clue

"You mean Sherlock's going to die?" Chet asked.

"It looks like it," Biff replied in a downcast voice.

All four went inside to speak to the doctor, a kindly-looking man in a white uniform.

"Don't be so glum, Biff," he said.

Biff's face brightened. "Is there some hope for my hound?"

"He's past the crisis," the vet replied.

"Good old gumshoe," Joe said.

Frank asked, "Can we take him with us now, Doc?"

"I'm afraid that's impossible. Sherlock's in no condition to travel."

"But we'll have to move on," said Joe.

Biff spoke up. "In that case I'll stay until the dog's ready to go and catch up with you later."

The boys looked at one another. Joe shrugged. "That'll be okay with me," he said.

"But," Chet said, "you can't carry a dog on a bus. I tried it once. No go."

"Leave the details to me," Biff said. "I'll get there somehow."

"Where will you stay while Sherlock's recuperating?" Frank inquired.

The vet smiled when he heard this. "Biff can help me around my hospital and in return he can have a bed in my home," he said. "The dog's recovery should only take a couple days."

"Thanks, Doc," Biff said, grinning. Then he turned to the Hardys and Chet. "So long, fellows. Good luck! Try to find Whip Lasher by the time we meet again."

It was decided that the trio would have breakfast, then go ahead to Denver and notify Biff where they were staying. The ride was uneventful except for the grandeur of the country which opened up before their eyes. Their car climbed upward to the mile-high city on the eastern slope of the Rockies. The air was crisp and clear and the city sparkled in the late-afternoon sunshine.

Chet poured over a map. He located a large camping site on the northern fringes of Denver and they pulled in between two other trailers. After the boys had set up their tent, the young couple on their right strolled over.

"Hi, my name's Henry," said the man. "This is my wife Betty."

Frank Hardy introduced his group and Henry went on, "You're just in time for the cook-off competition."

"What's that?" asked Chet.

"It's really something to see," Betty remarked. She told them that a soup company sponsored the Open-Fire Camp Cooking Contest. "Contestants' recipes are selected for main dish, vegetable, and dessert," she said.

As she spoke, the aroma of food drifted over the campsite, and the boys saw other people being drawn to the competition.

"We're going over now," Betty said. "Want to come along?"

Frank, Joe, and Chet joined the couple and walked to an area behind the campsite. Twenty or more campfires were burning and contestants with skillets, pots, and pans were nearly finished with their masterpieces.

A tall man wearing western boots and a ten-gallon hat spoke over a microphone. "Ladies and gentlemen! We have fifteen judges—seven men, seven women, and a little girl. But one of the fellows dropped out. Do we have a volunteer taster?"

"Here!" Joe cried out and lifted Chet's arm in the air.

"Wait a minute!" the stout boy protested.

"Ah-ha," the official called out. "That well-fed young man will be perfect."

Frank and Joe pushed Chet forward as the emcee went on, "What is your name?"

"Chet Morton."

"You'll be one of the dessert tasters."

A benign smile crossed Chet's face. Desserts were his favorites!

"I'm really in luck!" he told the Hardys.

The aroma of the cook-off was enough to make anybody hungry. The smoke which drifted over the area carried the scent of grilled trout, gingered ham in tantalizing juices, and Twirly Birds, a special chicken recipe. Frank and Joe followed Chet to a table marked *Desserts*.

"Look at these!" Chet exclaimed as he read the labels. "Caramel peach crunch, apple dumplings, and peach turnovers."

"Will the tasters eat sparingly of the sweets," the announcer said. "I'm saying this for your own good!"

Several men and women joined Chet as they sampled the luscious recipes. "Hm!" Chet mused. "Can't seem to make up my mind!" He went from dish to dish, taking a man-sized portion each time. His eyes rolled and he smacked his lips.

"Come on, Chet!" Joe prodded him as the onlookers chuckled.

"They're all so good," Chet said. "It's awfully hard to figure out which is best!"

"All right," Frank said. "Just one more time, fellow!"

Chet patted his stomach and started down the line again, relishing each mouthful. Finally he decided. "I vote for the caramel peach crunch," he said when the roll was called.

"Chet's in for trouble," Joe whispered to Frank. "Look, he's getting pale."

"I'd say he's getting green around the gills," Frank remarked.

Chet's smile had vanished. "Fellows," he said, "I'm going back to our trailer. How far is it?"

"About ten miles," Joe said.

"Don't say that!" Chet made his way through the crowd at a half-trot and held his stomach.

By the time Frank and Joe reached the camper, they found their buddy lying down.

"How do you feel, my gourmet friend?" Joe asked.

"Better."

But Chet's illness lasted the balance of the evening. In the morning he was still not his bouncy self.

"Want to come downtown with us?" Joe asked after breakfast.

"What for?"

Frank explained that they were going to visit the Mountain Dogie Store.

"Don't ask me to do anything for a while, will you?" Chet begged.

"Okay, you stay and recuperate," Frank said. "Joe and I will be back later."

With a nod of appreciation, Chet said good-by. The Hardys unhitched their car and drove to a public telephone, where they contacted Biff to tell him of their whereabouts. Sherlock was well enough to travel, Biff reported, and they would leave that morning. Then Frank and Joe went on to downtown Denver. It did not take long to find the Mountain Dogie Store. A sign announced: *The World's Greatest Emporium for Sports and Camping.*

The smell of new cloth and leather goods pervaded the huge store. Crowds moved about inspecting hundreds of items from camping gear to sports clothes.

At an information booth they obtained directions to the shoe department. Frank asked for the head clerk. He was a young man in his twenties.

"We'd like to know," Frank said, "if anybody recently bought shoes here with a Magnacard."

The young man was immediately interested. "I think we might have some information on that," he said. "You'll have to talk to the general manager. Follow me, please."

They went up a flight of stairs to an office located off the mezzanine. There they were introduced to a thin, balding middle-aged man named Jerrold Morris.

"They have a question about a Magnacard," the clerk said and excused himself.

Morris motioned the boys to be seated and

looked at them suspiciously. "Now what was that about a Magnacard?" he asked.

The Hardys identified themselves, explaining they were on the trail of Whip Lasher. "We're sure he bought a pair of shoes here," Frank concluded.

"Well, I don't know if it's the same man or not," Morris said, "but a fellow calling himself Robert Wheeler bought a pair of shoes a couple of months ago. Besides that, he outfitted himself with some of our best merchandise."

"On a phony Magnacard?" Frank queried.

"That's right. There was another man with him. I wish we could lay our hands on those two! The police are working on the case."

"Did you get a description of Wheeler and his companion?" Joe asked.

Morris nodded. "Our shoe clerk remembered Wheeler quite well."

Frank showed him the photograph.

"This could very well be the same fellow," Morris said.

"Did he leave any clues?" Joe wanted to know.

"No. We questioned our salesmen. They have no idea where the man was from or where he was going."

"What about the wrappers?" Frank asked.

Much to the Hardys' surprise, the packers had not been questioned.

"We would like to talk with them," Frank said.

"Sure."

Morris rose and led the way downstairs to an aisle in the back of the store where several women were busy packing merchandise. He asked if anyone remembered wrapping an order including a buckskin jacket and Mountain Dogie shoes, bought with a Magnacard charge plate. "This might be the man who purchased it," he said and passed the photo around.

One woman, Mrs. Jones, identified Wheeler from the picture. "Whenever I see Magnacard on the sales slip," she said, "I'm interested in the customer. We don't get millionaires down here very often."

"What did the other man look like?" Frank asked.

"Well, he was kind of chubby, and had dark hair. That's all I remember about him."

"Did they talk to each other while they were waiting?"

The woman frowned. "They mentioned a place called Foot Meadow a couple of times."

"Where's that?" Joe asked Morris.

"Never heard of it," the man replied.

"Neither have I," Mrs. Jones added.

"Well, thank you for your information," Frank said. "You may have been a big help to us."

"If you should capture those fellows, let me know," Morris said.

"Will do," Frank promised.

The boys returned to their car, then drove out of the store's parking lot into a busy street which led past the Brown Palace Hotel. Farther on, as they passed a jewelry shop, Frank jammed on the brakes.

"Joe, look!"

In front of the shop stood three familiar characters. Juice, Rip, and Fingers!

"Oh-oh," Joe said. "They followed us to Denver!"

"Wonder what they're doing in front of that shop," Frank said. He pulled up to the curb.

"I'd say they're trying to case the place." Joe glanced back and saw Fingers walk into the store while the others waited outside.

Joe looked at his brother. "Frank, do you suppose this is a stick-up?"

CHAPTER XI

A Shattering Experience

FRANK and Joe looked around for a policeman, but there was none in sight. So they hastened toward the jewelry store.

Frank said, "I'll go inside just in case there's trouble. You stay out here to cover me if those two guys try anything funny."

When Juice and Rip saw them coming, their mouths dropped open in surprise. Juice held a bottle of orange soda in his hand. Trying to be casual, he took a swig.

"What are you guys doing here?" Rip asked.

The Hardys did not reply. Joe stayed outside while Frank strode into the shop. Counters lined both sides and the far end, where Fingers, his back to the door, was talking to the clerk.

Quietly Frank stepped forward. Fingers reached into his jacket and pulled something out.

Frank edged closer. "Thank goodness," he said to himself, "it's not a holdup."

Fingers had a pouch in his hand. He opened it and shook several sapphires onto the velvet pad covering the glass counter. "Want to buy them?" he asked the clerk.

"Where'd you get these?"

"In the mountains. Blackfoot country."

The clerk picked up the stones one by one to examine them. "These weren't stolen?"

"No."

Suddenly, from the corner of his eye, Fingers spied Frank. He wheeled around and blanched. "What're you trailing me for?" he said.

"Who's trailing who?" Frank shot back.

Fingers looked at the clerk and said, "Excuse me a minute." He motioned Frank toward the front of the store.

"Look, you're going to spoil this whole deal for me!" he hissed.

"How can I spoil anything if you're on the up-and-up?"

"We'll talk about that later," Fingers replied. "Now leave me alone. I need some money."

"Okay." Frank stepped out into the sunlit street. There he found Joe being heckled by Juice and Rip.

"You've got nothing on us," Juice was saying.

With an innocent look, Joe said, "Of course not. You three guys are model citizens."

"Don't be wise," Rip said. "You'll get what's coming to you if you keep following us."

Frank spoke up. "It's a free country. We'll go anywhere we please."

Just then Fingers came out of the door, glowering. His forehead was lined with anger. "You blew it for me!" he muttered at Frank.

Joe noticed that Rip was edging closer to him. Suddenly Rip kicked viciously. Joe hopped nimbly aside and Rip's foot went through the plate-glass window.

It shattered as if hit by an explosion. The whole pane fell in, splintering over the display of jewelry and setting off the burglar alarm.

"Beat it!" Fingers cried out.

The trio raced down the street, dodging passers-by. A patrol car appeared and screeched to a halt. The clerk came racing from the store and a crowd hemmed in Frank and Joe.

An officer pushed through the milling throng and began to ask questions.

Joe related what had happened, and a man stepped forward to corroborate his story.

"Do you know where those fellows were headed?" the policeman asked the Hardys.

"No, sir."

"Okay, you can go. We'll look for them."

On their way back to the campsite, a thought suddenly leaped at Frank.

"Joe, Fingers mentioned Blackfoot country in the jewelry shop!"

"So?"

"Remember that wrapper in the Mountain Dogie Store said that Lasher and his pal had mentioned Foot Meadow?"

"Blackfoot Meadow!" Joe exclaimed.

"That could be it," Frank said. He pulled to the side of the road, grabbed the camping guide on the dashboard, and thumbed through the book. "Look, here it is!"

Frank pointed to the name Blackfoot Meadow. It was a public camping spot maintained by the State of Colorado, located in extremely rugged mountainous country.

"Just the place for a hideout," Joe said.

"We ought to drive there right away," Frank said.

"But what about Biff and Sherlock?"

"Guess we'd better wait here for them."

By this time Biff and his dog had already left the animal hospital and were on their way to the campsite. The two had not been able to get on a bus. On Biff's back was a cleverly devised sling made of an old bedsheet and in it rested Sherlock.

The hound's lugubrious visage looked out over Biff's shoulder as the sturdy young athlete walked along, trying to thumb a ride.

Several cars slowed down to look at the unusual sight, but continued on without stopping.

"Don't worry, Sherlock," Biff said. "We'll get

there. But I wish this was Be-Kind-to-Animals Week."

After several miles Biff put the dog down and Sherlock walked for ten minutes. The hot sun and the weakness caused by his recent illness brought the panting animal to a halt. Biff poured some water from his canteen into a tin dish and Sherlock lapped it up. Then the boy hoisted his pet onto his back again.

His right arm had gotten tired of thumbing when a car slowed down and stopped. In it were a man and a woman. "You poor boy!" the woman said after rolling down the window of the air-conditioned Ford. "What are you doing out here?"

"Trying to get to Denver with my dog," Biff replied.

"We'd like to give you a lift, but my husband is allergic to dogs."

"Anyway, it's nice of you to stop, ma'am," Biff said.

"Here, maybe this will help," the woman said. She reached into the back seat and pulled two sandwiches from a bag. Smiling, she handed them to Biff.

"Thank you," the boy said. "This will come in real handy."

The woman rolled up the window and the car sped on. Biff ate one sandwich, Sherlock the other.

"Okay, old chum," the boy said. "We're off again."

He trudged on under the blazing sun, but no one offered him a lift. Biff was beginning to feel discouraged when he spotted a car parked beside the road in a clump of cottonwood trees a quarter of a mile ahead.

As Biff approached, he saw that the hood was up and a man was tinkering with the motor.

He looked up and smiled at Biff. "Excuse me, I don't mean to laugh," he said with a thick German accent. "But I've never seen a boy before with a dog knapsack!"

"Man's best friend," Biff replied with a grin. "I'm sure Sherlock would do the same for me if he could. But he's just recuperating from a recent illness."

Biff put the dog down and looked at the motor. "Overheated?" he asked.

"No. I don't know what's the matter. Something in the ignition system, I think."

Biff had taken his own car apart and put it together several times. He studied the maze of wires carefully. "Sometimes a loose connection will cause trouble," he said.

"*Ja*, I was thinking that. Except that I cannot find anything loose."

"Tell you what," Biff suggested. "If I fix your car, will you take me to Denver?"

"And the *Hund*, too," the man said, smiling.

"Sure. He's my baggage."

Biff introduced himself and told his story. Then he found out that the stranded motorist was Fritz Burger from Austria. He was on a tour of the United States.

"I do a lot of climbing in the Alps, and I intend to see if your Rockies are as great a challenge," Burger said, watching Biff as he checked the automobile's wiring.

Finally Biff found the trouble. A cable beneath the low-slung car had been cut, as if by a sharp knife.

"Have you been over some rough ground?" Biff asked.

"*Ja.*"

"A sharp flying stone could have done this. I'll fix it."

"Thank you," Burger said with a grin. "Good thing you came along. Now we all go to Denver."

Biff expertly repaired the damage and soon they were on their way.

It was late afternoon when Burger pulled into the Hardys' camping spot.

"Biff, you made it!" Joe called out when he saw his friend approaching.

Frank and Chet came out and introductions were made. Burger said he would stay for the night and continue on the next morning.

"Where are you going?" Frank asked.

The Austrian explained that there were two

mountains he wanted to climb. "One is Eagle Ridge, the other Blackfoot Peak."

"That must be near Blackfoot Meadow!" Joe said. "We're headed there too!"

As he spoke, an object whizzed through the air, just missing Joe's head. It crashed into the side of the camper and burst to pieces!

CHAPTER XII

Prince Cuthbert

AT the sound of the crash everybody ducked. Splinters of glass fell on Joe's hair and he gingerly combed out the pieces.

The Austrian said, "You have enemies?"

"A few," Frank replied. He bent down to examine the larger pieces of glass. "Just as I thought!" he muttered. "An orange soda bottle. Juice probably threw it."

Leaving Biff and Burger, the Hardys and Chet fanned out over the area in an effort to locate the assailant.

"He's a pretty slippery guy," Frank remarked as they came to the edge of the camping area beside the highway.

"Look!" Chet said, pointing. "There's his trail bike!"

The motorcycle was parked a hundred yards away. As the Hardys approached, they could see the name Vampire Trail on it.

But before they had a chance to advance farther, a figure darted out of a huge drainpipe laid under the highway.

"There he goes!" Joe cried.

Juice was closer to the bike than the Hardys. Joe was only ten feet behind when Juice gave the machine gas, sending up a spray of dirt and gravel into Joe's face. He sped off down the road, waving defiantly.

"No use to chase after him now," Frank said as the youth zigzagged through the traffic and finally disappeared from sight.

When they returned to the camper, Biff was feeding Sherlock and chatting with Burger. The boys invited the Austrian to have supper with them and he gratefully accepted.

As they ate, the Hardys plied Burger with questions, mainly about his country. The man said he was an engineer and that his hobbies were travel and mountain climbing. "So now I try your American mountains," he said.

Biff remarked, "Fritz says Blackfoot Peak is dangerous."

"In what way?" Frank wanted to know.

Burger shrugged. "That I don't know, but I'll find out."

"Thanks again for helping Biff and Sherlock," Joe said. "In German I believe you say—*Danke schön!*"

"*Bitte schön,*" Burger replied with a grin.

"Gosh," Chet said, "I didn't know you could speak German, Joe."

Joe chuckled. "Picked it up on TV."

Burger said good night, adding that he hoped to see the boys again. But by the time they awakened the next morning, the Austrian's car was gone.

"Now let's see if we can have a peaceful day," Biff said, after he had exercised Sherlock and they were ready to depart.

"If we don't have any more trouble with that dog of yours, we should reach Blackfoot Meadow this evening," Frank said. He pulled out of the parking area and joined the sparse traffic on the mountain road.

After a short stop for lunch they set off again. The road led higher and higher, and the boys breathed deeply of the thin, exhilarating air.

"By the way," said Chet, who was munching a spare sandwich in the back seat, "when you find this guy Whip Lasher, what will you do with him?"

"Turn him over to the police," Joe said.

"Don't count your chickens before they've hatched," Frank put in. "We'll have to catch him first, and that won't be easy."

In the middle of the afternoon they drove down the main street of the village of Snowcap.

"Pretty snazzy," Biff remarked as he looked at the elegant stores lining both sides of the street.

Joe studied his guidebook. It stated that Snow-cap was an exclusive ski village in the winter, and in summer catered to vacationists at the many luxury dude ranches located in the surrounding area. It had a number of smart shops and fine restaurants.

"This is no place for us," Biff said. "Too rich for our blood."

"Who wants this ritzy stuff, anyhow?" Chet said. "We're the camper type. Let's go on."

The road switched back and forth as they climbed even higher. Finally it dipped into a broad, flat valley spreading open like a wide green carpet between two towering peaks. A sign announced: *Blackfoot Meadow State Park.*

All types of trailers dotted the cozy sites laid out along a stream shaded by willows and cotton-woods.

"What a great view," Frank said.

At the park entrance were a cluster of rustic shops and modern facilities for campers. Joe eyed the grocery store since they needed to stock up. Chet pointed to a laundromat.

"Look, you guys," he said. "I've got a couple of shirts that are a little gamey. Think I'll do some laundry."

"Okay, go ahead," Frank said. "I've got a few things to be washed, too."

"Same here," the others chimed in.

After they had found a pleasant camping spot,

the boys uncoupled the trailer tent and quickly set it up. While Frank and Joe went to the grocery store for supplies, Chet gathered up the clothes and took them to the laundromat.

He pushed through the door and looked around. Two women sat on folding chairs, watching their laundry tumble behind the glass doors of the machines. At the far end, a girl about Chet's age was bending over a half-filled basket of clothes.

Chet got a packet of soap powder from a vending machine and approached a machine with its door half open. Paying more attention to the girl than to the clothes in his hand, he stuffed them into the machine, tossed in the detergent, and closed the door. The machine began to whirl.

Suddenly the girl turned about. An expression of indignation covered her pretty face.

"You can't do that!" she cried out.

"Wh-what do you mean?" Chet asked. "Can't boys do laundry in this place?"

"Not in *my* machine!"

Chet looked bewildered as the girl chided him.

"Half of my laundry was in the machine you're using!" she told him rather sharply.

Chet blushed. "Gee, I'm sorry. I didn't see it!" He was embarrassed and sat down on the bench, looking glum.

"Oh, don't take it so hard," the girl said finally. "There's no harm done."

Encouraged, Chet brightened and began to tell

her about his friends and the camping trip. "You see, we're detectives," he said importantly. "And we're looking for a crook called Whip Lasher."

"What an odd name," the girl said.

"He's one of the country's most wanted swindlers." Chet went into great detail in describing the suspect, including the buckskin jacket.

The girl said, "Several men around here wear buckskin jackets. One of them could be the one you're looking for."

"Oops, the wash is done," Chet said.

"I'll dry it for you," the girl offered.

When it was ready, Chet raced back to the camper. Frank and Joe were stowing away the canned goods they had bought.

"We've got hamburgers and hot dogs too, Chet," Joe said.

"And I've got a clue!" Chet exulted. "A couple of guys in this camp are wearing buckskin jackets. One of them could be Whip Lasher!"

"Calm down," Biff said. "Buckskin jackets are a fad right now, Chet old boy. Don't jump to conclusions."

Chet passed out the laundry. "Okay. But I'll bet if you let old Sherlock smell that inner sole he'll pick up the scent!"

"Good idea!" Frank replied.

He produced the inner sole and the sad-eyed hound sniffed at it. Then Biff attached a leash and led Sherlock outside.

They walked leisurely about the meadow, chatting briefly with some of the campers who made admiring comments about the dog. Sherlock paused to sniff several spots, but then disdainfully padded away. As they passed an equipment store which sold and rented trail bikes, Sherlock became interested in a new scent and strained at the leash.

"He's on the trail, Frank!" Biff exclaimed.

They walked rapidly behind the hound who kept his nose to the ground, with ears flapping. He stopped beside the steps of a small trailer. It was weirdly painted in psychedelic colors.

The dog moved around in circles as if he had lost the scent. Did Lasher get into a car at this spot or was he inside the trailer? Joe pressed close to the screen door and looked in. What he saw of the dim interior was even more weird than the exterior.

The walls were covered with paintings and tapestries. Colored tassels hung down from the corners of the ornate picture frames. Two rows of bookshelves were set high above a silk-covered couch laden with embroidered pillows.

Joe turned to the others. "This is fantastic," he said.

Just then a voice boomed out, "Who's there?"

The Hardys gulped and Frank stepped forward. "Just some curious visitors, sir."

"Then come in."

Frank motioned to the others to wait, then he opened the door and stepped inside. As his eyes became accustomed to the dimness, he saw the robed figure of a man seated in a thronelike chair at the rear of the trailer.

He had a full beard, squared off at the bottom. His mustache was waxed, with each end standing straight up like a spear. On his head was a jewel-studded Norman-style helmet made of cloth. Several medals were pinned to his velvet jacket and rings sparkled on his fingers.

Frank's gaze met the keen blue eyes of the regal-looking occupant. "I'm—I'm Frank Hardy," the boy said.

"Pleased to meet you. My name is Prince Cuthbert de Solo Prudham du Paris."

"Oh. Do you always dress like this?"

"Indeed I do, as befits royalty." The man's piercing eyes never wavered. "You see, I'm a direct descendant of King Arthur and the lawful prince of the British Isles and Normandy."

"That's quite an honor," Frank commented with a straight face. He glanced about, but saw no sign of Whip Lasher. "Nice to meet you, Prince," Frank said as he backed toward the door.

"I suppose you're a camper, too," the prince went on. "New to these parts?"

"Yes, sir. We'll be here for a day or two."

"My advice is to beware of Vampire Trail!"

The same name as Juice Barden's trail bike!

"What's Vampire Trail?" Frank asked casually.

Prince Cuthbert explained that it was a path leading to the top of Blackfoot Peak. "Don't go there," he warned. "It's very dangerous—vampire bats and the like!"

"Thank you," Frank said and hastened outside.

He beckoned Joe, Chet, and Biff to follow him. When they were a discreet distance from the trailer, Frank burst out laughing.

"Wow! You should have seen that guy who lives in there! A real wacky eccentric who thinks he's related to King Arthur!" Frank told the boys about his conversation with the man and they chuckled.

"Did you ask him about Whip Lasher and show him the picture?" Joe asked.

"No. He might be in with Lasher, for all we know."

"And what about Vampire Trail?"

Frank shrugged. "We'll have to find out what's going on there."

Biff spoke up. "Suppose I rent a trail bike and explore that Vampire Trail while you look for Whip Lasher."

"Okay," said Frank.

Biff left the bloodhound with Chet and hurried off to rent a motorbike.

"Don't be too long," Chet called to Biff. "Dinner's at seven!"

A further search of Blackfoot Meadow turned

up no trace of Lasher. Questions put to shop-keepers and campers elicited only negative replies.

"How about rustling up some grub?" Frank asked Chet when they returned to the trailer.

Biff had not come back yet. Chet cooked the hamburgers and set out the tasty repast. "If Biff doesn't show up soon, he just won't get any," he declared.

It was after dusk when a car pulled up beside the boys' camper. A trail bike was lashed to the top. Out stepped Fritz Burger. He walked around to the other door, opened it, and helped Biff to his feet.

"Biff! Fritz! What's the matter?" Frank exclaimed.

"Your friend was attacked on Vampire Trail," Burger said.

Biff shook his head groggily, and Chet noticed a red welt on his neck.

"A vampire bite!" Chet moaned.

CHAPTER XIII

A Grizzly Attack?

By the time Biff had completely recovered, Fritz Burger was on his way again to Blackfoot Peak.

Biff said, "I was dry-gulched by somebody. Wow! I didn't know what hit me!"

"It was the vampire bat!" Chet said. "Remember what Prince Cuthbert told Frank."

"There aren't any vampire bats in this part of the world," Frank declared. "They're found in warmer climates like Central America. I think this vampire bat had two legs!"

The Hardys were determined to pursue the matter further. Next morning they sought out a forest ranger who had an information booth next to the grocery store. He was brown-haired and slender, and told them he was a graduate student who worked there in the summer. His name was Herb Johnson.

Frank brought up the subject of Vampire Trail and asked if there had been any previous trouble in that area.

"Why, what happened?" Johnson asked.

"One of the fellows with us got clobbered there last evening," Frank replied.

Johnson shook his head. "Funny thing about that place. You know, the real name is not Vampire Trail at all, it's Grizzly Trail. But alleged recent vampire bat attacks prompted the nickname."

The ranger shook his head. "I thought the bats were merely a figment of the campers' imagination."

"The attack on our friend was not imaginary," Frank said and mentioned the welt on Biff's neck.

"Could it have been a mosquito or spider bite?"

"Hardly. By the way, have you ever been up there?" Joe asked.

"Yes, a couple of years ago. Two other students and I went up on a grizzly bear survey."

Herb related his experience. They had anaesthetized several bears with darts and tagged them for future observation.

"We'd like to go up, too," Frank said.

"I suppose you could make it. But look out for those grizzlies. One swipe with a paw and you've had it!"

The ranger promised to report the attack on

Biff to his supervisors. "We'll have to send a group up and see who's prowling around," he said.

When Frank and Joe returned to the camper, they found Chet in a peevish mood. "This place is getting too crowded," he complained. "Trailers here, trailers there. Didn't we come out here to enjoy the wide-open country?"

"You've got a point," Biff agreed. "I'm afraid Sherlock might get run over in all this traffic."

"Okay," Joe said. "Let's pull out."

They decided to drive up Blackfoot Pass Road until they found an isolated spot not too far from the main camping facilities. Quickly the trailer was folded up. Then the rented bike was secured over the trailer hitch. The caravan moved slowly out of the park and onto the highway leading through Blackfoot Pass.

After Frank had driven about a mile, Biff said, "Vampire Trail is up ahead to the right."

Frank slowed down. Dense foliage hung over the trail which showed scant evidence of use. Years ago it probably had been used as a logging road.

Joe was surveying the area to the left. The hills sloped gradually to a spot sheltered by a screen of pine trees.

"Let's camp up there," he suggested. "That's plenty private."

"Good idea," Biff agreed. "Then we can keep an eye on Vampire Trail."

"Okay," said Frank. He turned left and drove across the shoulder of the road, then carefully wound his way upward among the trees and low bushes. When he stopped, they were about fifty feet from the road, looking down at a thirty-degree angle.

"Boy, we're hidden and yet we can see everything!" Chet chortled.

He and Biff offered to set up the camper, while Frank and Joe rode the bike back to the trailer park to continue the search for Whip Lasher. When purple shadows began to creep into the meadow, the Hardys decided to return to their campsite.

Chet was busy with the skillet when they arrived. "We had a nice quiet afternoon," he stated. "A little snooze and plenty to eat."

"Did anyone go up Vampire Trail while we were gone?" Joe asked.

"No," Chet replied.

Biff, who had hiked through the woods with Sherlock, had nothing to report either besides sighting four startled deer.

Shortly after they had gone to bed, the boys heard the put-put of a trail bike. Frank and Joe scrambled out of their sleeping bags and ran to look through the pine trees down to the road below.

"It's going up Vampire Trail," Joe said.

The bike's lamps bobbed and swerved along the

rough, twisting trail. Finally the light disappeared from view.

"Come on, Joe. Let's follow."

It was agreed that Chet and Biff would guard the trailer while the Hardys went up the mountain. They dressed hurriedly, took their flashlights, and started up the trail. The sound of the bike's motor grew fainter.

After several hundred yards, Frank paused. "Joe, listen. Do you hear anything?"

Except for the rhythmic song of the peepers the woods were silent.

"The bike has stopped," Joe declared. "In that case, we've got to be very careful. Let's not walk together."

They split up, Frank taking the left side of the trail, Joe the right. They moved along quietly, using their flashlights as sparingly as possible. Occasionally they signaled each other by winking the lights briefly.

The trail became steep. Frank climbed over a low boulder and slipped. With a grunt he landed on his stomach. Had there been another outcry at the same time? Frank was not sure. When he regained his footing, he flashed to signal Joe. There was no return blink!

Frank's heart pounded. Dared he risk discovery by calling out to his brother? He flashed again. Still no response.

Frank crawled to the opposite side of the path

and began a methodical search—from the edge of the trail twenty feet into the dense woods and back again. "Joe, where are you?" he whispered hoarsely.

All was silent. Frank reasoned that if he continued to search alone he, too, might be assailed by the unknown enemy. It would be more practical if Biff and Chet joined in the hunt.

Frank hurried to the trailer and told the others what had happened.

"What if the vampire bats got Joe!" Chet cried.

"Sherlock will find Joe," Biff said.

He let the dog sniff the boy's sleeping bag. Then they set off. This time they did not take the precaution of dousing their flashlights. Speed was essential.

After a while Frank said, "It was right about here that I slipped."

"Look, there's Joe!" Biff exclaimed.

The boy lay in the middle of the trail. Hearing the others, he sat up groggily. Sherlock went up and licked his face.

"Joe, what happened?" Frank asked as he and Biff helped his brother to his feet.

"Remember when you slipped?" Joe said. "Just then I heard a rustling behind me. I was kayoed by a blow across my back."

"Was it a bear?" Biff inquired.

"No. Whoever walloped me carried me up here to the middle of the trail."

"Let's look at your neck," Chet said. He shone his light on the open collar of Joe's shirt. *There was a red welt!*

"What'd I tell you?" Chet quavered. "The vampire bat struck again!"

Joe regained his strength gradually. By the time they reached the foot of the mountain, he was matching strides with the other three. Back at the camp, Chet applied medication to the welt.

It was hard to settle down for the night. All were too excited about what had happened. Frank said, "Somebody must be camping on the trail."

"That's what I think," Joe agreed. "It might be a hideout for Whip Lasher and the other credit-card crooks."

"That's right," Biff said. "They're sportsmen, aren't they?"

"Great sports!" Chet muttered. "When they hit you and you're not looking!"

The boys listened for an hour, but there were no sounds of the trail bike returning.

"If it's up there, we're going to find it!" Joe vowed.

"You can say that again," Frank said.

After breakfast the next morning Frank decided to report the attack on Joe to the forest ranger, Herb Johnson. He and Biff cycled to Blackfoot Meadow, but the ranger was not at the information booth. On the counter were maps of the area. Frank took one.

As he turned to show it to Biff, his eyes lighted on a fringed buckskin jacket. The man wearing it was hurrying across an open area toward a trailer parked among the trees.

"That could be Whip Lasher!" Frank exclaimed. "Come on, Biff!"

But instead of going to the trailer, the man in the fringed jacket waved at a car driving past. It stopped to pick him up, then drove out of the park toward Snowcap.

Frank and Biff ran to their bike, jumped on, and followed. It irked Frank that he had not gotten a look at the man in the buckskin jacket. He gave the cycle full throttle and it gained on the car ahead.

Suddenly the motor began to sputter. They slowed down and came to a halt beside the road.

"Oh nuts!" Frank said. "It would conk out just now!"

"Sounds as if there's dirt in the fuel line," Biff said. He opened a small tool kit slung under the seat and soon found the source of the trouble. "Dirty gasoline, just as I thought," he added.

Quickly he cleaned the fuel line, then the boys set off again. By the time they reached Snowcap, the trail had been lost completely.

"No telling where they went," Frank said as he stopped on the main street.

"My guess is that Mr. Buckskin is right here in Snowcap," Biff said.

"The vampire bat struck again!" Chet quavered

"Could be. Let's take a look around."

The boys walked up and down the streets. Although they saw several men wearing buckskin, none was the notorious Whip Lasher.

Frank decided to take this opportunity to question local merchants about the Magnacard. Going from one shop to another, he asked discreetly if the owner had any trouble with Magnacard holders and presented Lasher's picture.

He was told that some clients had Magnacards, but there had been no swindles. At Burn's Jewelry Shop, however, the proprietor said he would take no more Magnacards.

"Did you get stuck?" Biff asked.

The jeweler nodded. "Someone bought a big sapphire from me on a Magnacard which proved to be fake." A hard look came over his face. "When I get hold of that crook, he's going to pay for it!"

"You'll have to leave that up to the police," Frank said. He pulled out Lasher's photo. "Is this the man?"

Burn studied it intently. "No."

"Can you describe the swindler?"

"Well, his face was round, too. Like this fellow in the photograph. But his hairline was higher. He was dark-haired and not very tall."

"What was the name on the Magnacard?"

"Minks. John Minks."

"By the way," Frank went on, "where do you buy your sapphires?"

The man seemed startled by the question. He forced a smile and replied, "That's my professional secret!"

CHAPTER XIV

Death Warrant

On the way back to their camp Frank called out over the rushing wind, "What do you make of this, Biff?"

"Strange that Burn wouldn't tell us where he got the sapphire. Maybe he bought it from Fingers!"

"I wonder where Fingers got those stones."

"So do I. As far as Minks is concerned," Biff said, "no doubt he's one of Lasher's gang."

They decided to stop at the state park grocery store to buy some bottles of soda. As they turned into the entrance, they saw Joe leaning against the Hardys' car.

Frank stopped. "What are you doing here?"

"Looking for Chet and Sherlock," Joe replied with a look of exasperation. He explained that they had driven the car into camp after Frank and

Biff had not come back, thinking they might need some help.

"What happened to you?" Joe asked. "We couldn't find you anywhere."

Frank told about the latest developments, then added, "So now Chet's lost?"

"Don't worry," Biff said. "He must be around somewhere. Just ask the campers if they've seen a left tackle with a hound dog."

They followed Biff's suggestion. Several people indicated that they had seen Chet near the psychedelic trailer! The trio walked up to it and Joe knocked on the door.

"Come in," Chet called out. They entered.

There sat Chet in Prince Cuthbert's chair. On his head was the jeweled helmet. Beside him on a velvet cushion lay Sherlock.

"Chet, are you out of your ever-loving skull?" Joe demanded.

Chet grinned benignly. "Lower your voice when speaking to royalty," he said with a wave of his hand.

"What's this all about?" Frank asked.

"I'm minding the trailer while His Highness is out on an errand. And you know what he's giving me for doing it?"

"No, what?"

"Half the city of London!"

"You're in the money," Joe quipped. "What are you going to do with half of London?"

"Quit ribbing me. You know that old geezer doesn't have all his marbles."

"I'm beginning to have my doubts about you, Chet," Frank said. "What's all this business with the fancy helmet?"

"I was wondering what it feels like to be a descendant of King Arthur," Chet replied.

"Aside from all that nonsense," Joe said, "I don't trust the prince."

"I think he's harmless enough," Frank put in.

The Hardys and Biff left Chet and resumed their search for Whip Lasher, on the chance he had returned to the campsite. Two hours later they went back to Prince Cuthbert's trailer. Chet was impatient.

"He said he'd be back soon," the boy moaned, glancing at his watch. "I didn't know he was going to *abdicate!*"

Biff laughed. "In that case, that makes you the lord and master!"

Just then the door handle turned and the prince entered. "Sorry—so sorry," he said.

"You took a long time," said Chet, removing the jeweled headpiece. "Where were you?"

"In Snowcap."

"Oh," Joe said. "Were you hobnobbing with American aristocracy?"

"No, none of that," Prince Cuthbert replied testily. "I was trying to sell some gems to a jeweler."

Frank asked quickly, "Are they sapphires?"

"Yes. How did you know?"

"Just a guess. Did you sell them?"

"My venture ended in complete failure," the prince replied. "The jeweler said he had plenty of sapphires."

"What a pity," said Joe, his eyes narrowing suspiciously. "My mother wants a sapphire for her birthday. Let's see what you have to offer."

Cuthbert took a pouch from his pocket and dropped several stones into the palm of his hand. They were uncut, the kind that Fingers had in his guitar.

Joe studied them carefully, then looked the prince straight in the eye and asked, "Where did you get these?"

"I bought them at a bargain."

"From whom?" Joe pressed.

"Three lads I met here at the park," Cuthbert answered. "They were an odd assortment." The eccentric went on to describe the Terrible Trio perfectly.

Joe rolled his eyes. "So they're here, too!"

"They just won't give up," Biff said.

"You know them?" the prince asked.

"We're acquainted," Frank said. He had an idea and asked Biff to get Sherlock. The tall boy stepped outside to bring in the dog.

One of the sapphire peddlers, Cuthbert said, had sat in the overstuffed chair in a corner of the trailer. Biff let Sherlock sniff the cushion. Then the boys thanked the prince for his information and left.

"Okay, Sherlock," Biff said. "Get busy!"

The dog's ears flapped as he zigzagged about, sniffing one scent, then another. Finally he found the trail of the person who had sat in the chair.

Sherlock strained at the leash, and the boys followed him across the campground. The dog led them out of the area and into a wooded section.

"It's getting late," Chet declared. "I hope we find those guys soon. I'm getting hungry."

Tire marks were evident on a path which led deeper into a pine woods. Frank and Joe studied the ground, finally locating the spot where a vehicle had turned off the trail.

Sherlock made the turn. "They can't be very far ahead," Biff said. "We'd better be quiet."

It was decided that Frank and Joe would go on ahead, while Chet and Biff remained behind with Sherlock. If the dog should bark, he would give away their position.

Moving from tree to tree, the Hardys finally spied the trailer. "Ha, we found the culprits," Joe whispered.

They crept as close as possible to the trailer without risking being seen. Voices came from inside. One belonged to Fingers. He said, "Listen, Pick! Let us work for you again. We won't steal anything this time!"

A deep voice replied, "I can't trust you. You take too many of the stones."

Juice retorted, "Suppose we tell the cops about this thing?"

Pick replied coldly, "That would be your death warrant. Now scram out of this territory!"

"We will," Fingers said, "if you give us a few more stones. We're broke."

"Okay. Here," came the reply.

Then a door slammed and the Hardys ducked for cover. A short, stocky man left the trailer and vanished into the woods in the opposite direction from which the boys had come. He moved so fast that Frank and Joe could not get a look at his face.

Seconds later there came the sound of a motor-bike, but it was too far away for the Hardys to follow.

They hastened back to where they had left Chet, Biff, and Sherlock. "Fingers and his pals are definitely involved in a crooked deal," Joe said and told what they had overheard.

"I wonder what they're up to," said Chet.

"And who is this character Pick?" Biff added.

"First thing to do is notify the police about those goons," Frank suggested.

Before leaving the public campsite, he put in a phone call to the Denver authorities, giving the location of the suspects' trailer and car.

Then the four took their car and the motorbike and returned to the trailer tent. After supper the

Hardys decided to scout Vampire Trail, but with sufficient equipment to spend the whole night if necessary.

"What can I do?" Biff asked.

After a discussion it was decided that Biff should spy on the Terrible Trio. Chet, meanwhile, would remain and guard their camp with Sherlock.

Frank and Joe took sleeping bags and a small amount of food.

"Good luck," Chet said. "And watch out for vampire bats!"

The Hardys picked their way carefully up the treacherous path. Night had settled and an eerie silence pervaded the woodland, broken every now and then by the spine-chilling call of a hoot owl.

The boys had been trudging along for nearly an hour when an unearthly cry rent the black stillness of the forest. They hastened toward the place from which the sound had come. This time they stayed close together for their mutual protection.

Suddenly Frank stepped on something squishy. He bent over, shone his light on the ground, and picked up a creature about three inches long. It had pointed ears and a horrid-looking face.

"A vampire bat!" Frank hissed, dropping it to the ground. As he did, another shriek sounded down the trail!

CHAPTER XV

A Terrified Escapee

HAD the cries come from a human being or from a trapped animal? The third time the Hardys heard the chilling shriek there was no doubt that it was the voice of a terrified man.

Frank and Joe strained their eyes to see through the darkness. Suddenly they made out the figure of a man, lumbering along, wheezing as if his lungs would burst.

Other footsteps sounded behind him, accompanied by muttered curses.

"He's being chased," Frank whispered to Joe. "We've got to save him!"

The boys sprang toward the startled man. Each seized an arm and they dragged him into the concealment of the forest and dived down behind a huge boulder.

Joe put a handkerchief over the man's mouth

to mute his labored breathing. Seconds later two pursuers charged past them up the trail. The boys waited tensely until the angry voices disappeared into the night. When they felt it was safe, they shone their lights on the fugitive.

His eyes rolled and he gasped for breath. Frank judged him to be about forty years old. He had a plump face and thin black hair covered his head in streaks. His jacket and trousers, of fashionable-cut, were ripped from his flight up Vampire Trail.

"Who are you? What's your name?" Frank asked.

"Wait . . . not . . . now . . . later."

"He's in no condition to talk yet," Joe said. "Let's take him back to camp."

The Hardys helped the man to his feet, lifting his arms over their shoulders. Thus supporting him, they half carried, half dragged him down Vampire Trail. Periodically they stopped and listened to make sure the man's pursuers were not returning.

When they came to Blackfoot Pass Road, the boys stopped. Leaving Joe with the man, Frank scouted the road for a hundred yards in each direction, making sure that no one was lying in wait. Then the Hardys assisted the stranger up the hill to their camp. Chet was wide-eyed with surprise when he saw them.

"Make room on Biff's bunk," Frank told him. "This man is nearly dead from exhaustion."

The stranger gratefully accepted the boys' kindness. After two pillows had been propped under his head, his breathing quieted to near normal. He began to answer questions.

"My name is Farkus," he said. "I'm a financier." He rolled to one side, fumbled for his wallet, and showed identification.

"What was going on up that trail?" asked Joe.

Farkus said that he had been kidnapped by three men in Snowcap.

"Why?" Frank inquired.

"I don't know. I think they were taking me up there to kill me!"

Farkus explained that he had been transported in a car as far up the trail as possible. When it had stopped, he dashed out and started to scramble ahead. "If you boys hadn't grabbed me, it would have been the end," he concluded.

The Hardys reasoned that the third man must have remained in the car, and had driven away before they had descended the trail again.

Chet confessed that he had been asleep for a while and had heard nothing.

Frank said, "Mr. Farkus, when you pull yourself together, we'll take you to the police. Things are getting pretty rough around here."

Farkus sat up on the edge of the bunk, shaking. "No! No! You can't do that!"

"But it's for your own protection, sir," said Chet.

The man pleaded not to be taken to the police. "Those kidnappers will kill me if they find out," he said. "Let me handle it my own way. I'll report it, but later."

Mention of the police seemed to have unnerved Farkus even more and Frank grew suspicious about the man's protestations. Farkus' hands moved around the bunk as if searching for a lost article.

"What's the matter?" asked Joe. "Did you drop something?"

"No—no. I'm just afraid of spiders. That's all," the man replied.

Frank and Joe stepped outside and discussed the stranger in low voices. "I think he has something to do with all those mysterious happenings on Vampire Trail," Frank said.

"On the other hand," said Joe, "maybe he's innocent. If he's a financier, perhaps the kidnappers were holding him for ransom."

Their minds tired from speculation, the young sleuths prepared for bed. They woke up occasionally and looked at Biff's bunk, half expecting that Farkus had gone. Near daybreak both boys fell into a deep slumber. They were awakened by the sound of sizzling bacon. Chet and Farkus were already up, and although the financier glanced about the woodland suspiciously, his face had lost the terror of the night before.

"You picked a good camping spot," he remarked.

"Yes," Chet agreed. "We can see what's happening on the trail."

"Oh? You have a special interest in that path?"

"Ow!" Chet cried as some grease spattered on his hand. "Not really—I mean, it's just supposed to be a dangerous place, that's all."

After breakfast Farkus stretched and yawned, saying that he would like to step outside for a breath of fresh air. Joe accompanied him.

Inside the camper, Frank cautioned Chet not to say anything more about Vampire Trail. "This guy Farkus could be in with the crooks," he said, adding, "The trail's a lot more dangerous than you think. I found a dead vampire bat last night!"

Chet, who was drying the skillet, let it clatter to the floor. "A real vampire bat?"

"A dead one. It was a scary-looking thing."

"I don't want to see any," Chet quavered.

Just then Biff came up the hill, pushing his trail bike. He was surprised to see Joe chatting with the stranger, and after being introduced, he went into the camper.

"What goes with that fat guy?" he asked.

Frank told him briefly what happened and said, "How about the Terrible Trio?"

"Still there," Biff replied. "I overheard them say that they'd stay for a while. So I thought I'd come back."

Frank nodded. Then he told Biff and Chet that he and Joe would take Farkus back to Snowcap.

"Okay," said Chet. "Meanwhile, we'll take a ride down to the park campsite and see what's going on."

The Hardys got into the front seat while Farkus slid into the back. As they passed the camping park, Joe, who was at the wheel, looked into the rear-view mirror. Farkus was hunched down in his seat as if to avoid being seen. The man kept silent all the way to Snowcap.

"Well, here we are," Frank said as Joe pulled up to the curb not far from Burn's Jewelry Store.

"Don't—don't stop here," Farkus begged. "Go down a little farther to my motel."

Joe continued on until Farkus pointed to a motel set back from the street. He pulled into the semicircular driveway.

"Thanks," Farkus said. He jumped out of the car and dashed into Room 14.

Joe drove back onto the street and out of sight of the motel. He parked and the two walked back.

"We'll check on him," Frank said. "Maybe his name isn't Farkus and maybe he isn't a financier."

The desk clerk in the motel office was friendly. He answered their questions, saying that Room 14 was rented to a man named A. Larson.

"Thanks," Frank said. "We thought it was someone we knew." Outside, he took his brother's arm. "Did you get that, Joe? A. Larson—the same initials as Archibald Lasher!"

CHAPTER XVI

Royal Trouble

"WHAT do you know!" said Joe. "So our friend Farkus is possibly tied up with Lasher. Maybe he's one of the gang!"

"Let's find a cop to make the arrest," said Frank.

The boys hurried up the main street, looking for a policeman. They could not locate one. Finally Frank said, "I wonder if there's a police station in this town."

"Let's ask someone," Joe suggested. They stepped into a haberdashery, where the clerk looked them up and down.

"We're not here to buy anything," Frank said. "But we'd like to know if there's a policeman in Snowcap."

"Why? Did you run into trouble?"

Frank did not reply. Instead he said, "You have a police station, don't you?"

"Hardly. The State Police usually takes care of our criminals—and bums."

"Don't get snooty with us," Joe said. "We're campers."

The boys left the store and went into a tearoom several doors away. The woman at the cashier's counter was polite and answered their questions.

"Yes, Snowcap has one policeman," she said. "He's usually at the information booth a block away. The town, however, has no jail." Beaming, she added, "We have very fine people here."

When they were on the street again, Joe snorted. "Fine people like Lasher and his cronies!"

"And if we don't find that policeman soon, they'll get away!" Frank stormed.

The town's lone police officer was seated on a chair outside the information booth. Frank told him of their suspicions. Talking slowly, the officer agreed to accompany the boys to the motel. His gait was even slower than his speech. To the impatient Hardys it seemed like hours before they reached the motel.

The policeman asked to see the occupant in Room 14.

"There's no one in there now," the clerk said. "Mr. Larson and his friend left a few minutes ago."

"You mean there were two men in Room 14?"

"That's right. Mr. Larson and Mr. Farkus."

Frank pulled out Lasher's photo. "Is he one of them?"

"Yes. That's Mr. Larson."

"May we look the room over?" Frank asked.

The clerk shrugged. "As long as the law's with you."

The officer stood by the open door while the Hardys looked around for clues. The wastebasket had been emptied. A search of the drawers and closets proved fruitless, too. Finally Joe glanced at the memo pad next to the telephone. Nothing was written on it, but the young detective's sharp eyes noticed indentations on the paper. He tilted the pad up to the light, then set it back again.

"Okay, nothing here," he said as they stepped outside. They thanked the officer and left.

Nearing their car, Joe said, "Frank, there *was* something on that pad!" He told of the indented letters. "They spelled Mungo!"

"Wow! The entire gang may be meeting at that motel," Frank said.

"Which means we may be able to catch the whole bunch," Joe said hopefully.

"I doubt it. They've been warned by Farkus and cleared out."

Frank headed west. Halfway to Blackfoot Meadow the Hardys saw Biff Hooper racing toward them on the trail bike. He waved frantically and Frank stopped. Biff pulled over beside him. He lifted the visor of his riding helmet and exclaimed, "Something awful has happened!"

"You look as if you've been in an earthquake," said Joe.

"It was more like a tornado. You should have seen the place."

"What place?" asked Frank. "For Pete's sake, calm down and tell us what's happened."

"Prince Cuthbert's trailer—somebody raided it. They bound, gagged, and blindfolded the poor old guy and ransacked the interior."

"I wonder what they were looking for," Frank mused.

Biff shrugged. "Who knows? Maybe they thought his jewels were real!"

The Hardys decided to visit Cuthbert and ask him a few questions. Biff followed them into the campground. When they reached the gaily painted trailer, they learned that the park police had already been there and left.

The prince's quarters were still in disorder. When the boys entered, he was trying to hang the pictures back on the tapestried walls. Then he adjusted his helmet, set his throne back on the small dais from which it had toppled, and seated himself.

"I must not forget that I am royalty," he said, "despite the adversities which have beset me."

"I've got to hand it to you," said Biff. "You're taking this mighty calmly."

The prince raised his hand. "I shall send word

to my retainers. They will hasten from Europe and track down the assailants."

"Tell us what happened," Frank said. "What were your attackers looking for?"

Cuthbert said that in the middle of the night someone forced the door. Two men entered, and before he had a chance to sit up, they bound and gagged him. The prince had not seen them, because they blindfolded him before turning on the lights.

"Did they take anything?" Frank asked.

"Only those sapphires I had. That's what amazes and confounds me. My crown jewels, worth much more, were untouched. Even the royal documents were overlooked by those scoundrels."

With Cuthbert's permission the boys searched for clues but found none. Frank advised the prince to get a stronger lock for his door. Then the young detectives stepped outside and walked over to a Coke machine.

"Who do you think robbed the prince?" Joe asked.

"He must have told other people about those sapphires," Frank said. "Perhaps Fingers and his gang came back to steal them."

They were finishing their refreshing drinks when Chet Morton approached at a trot with Sherlock on a leash.

"Here, have a drink," said Joe. He produced

another bottle and handed it to the perspiring boy.

Chet took a long swig, wiped the back of his hand across his mouth, and pulled something from his pants pocket. "Another clue," he declared, handing a Magnacard to Frank. It was made out to John Minks.

"So Farkus swindled the jeweler!" Frank exclaimed. "Burn's description fits him, too! "Where'd you get this, Chet?"

"In our camper. I was cleaning up the place and found it under Biff's bunk. Figured our friend Farkus dropped it."

"I don't think he dropped it," Joe said.

"What do you mean?" Chet asked.

"I think he hid it when he showed us the identification in his wallet. Then he couldn't find it again. Remember how he was looking around, saying he was afraid of spiders?"

"That was a lot of baloney, all right," Frank declared.

"Anyway, it throws a different light on the mystery," Joe said.

The four discussed the new development. Perhaps Farkus had not been kidnapped at all. Maybe the two pursuers were enemies and he had been racing up Vampire Trail to reach the protection of his own gang!

"That Magnacard bunch could have a hideout at the top of the mountain," Joe stated.

Biff snapped his fingers. "Maybe they manufacture the cards there!"

"Could be," said Joe.

Frank pocketed the charge plate and they returned to their car. Chet got in back with the dog, while Biff mounted the bike for the ride back to their camp.

"It's past chow time," Chet complained.

"Okay, you can whip something up real quick," Joe said.

The thought of juicy hamburgers made Chet's stomach grumble. "Come on, Joe! Can't you go a little faster? I'm dying of hunger."

The car hummed along the highway between the towering green walls of Blackfoot Pass. Finally they veered left up the hill to their campsite.

"Boy, our trailer sure is well hidden," Chet said as they neared the spot. "You can't even see it from here."

Joe drove a little farther, then cried out, "I'll say you can't. It's gone!"

CHAPTER XVII

An Unexpected Denial

CHET fumed. "The Terrible Trio stole it, that's who!"

"Somebody sure doesn't want us near Vampire Trail," Frank remarked. He glanced about for a clue to the thief or thieves.

There was nothing but tracks made by the wheels of their camper. Apparently it had been pulled down to the road before being hitched onto a car.

"Where do we start looking?" Biff asked.

Frank said there were three possibilities. The thieves could have driven east or west along Blackfoot Pass Road, or up Vampire Trail. The latter, however, showed no sign of fresh car tracks.

"Biff, you and Chet ride the cycle back to Blackfoot Meadow," Frank said. "Joe and I will drive west over the pass."

"Good luck," Biff called out. "We'll meet back here."

"Okay." Frank stepped on the gas. As Blackfoot Pass Road ascended, the valley became narrower and more twisted. The boys checked both sides of the road for a sign of their camper, but in vain.

Near the top of the pass was a turnout cut into a rock wall looming thirty feet high on the left. Much to Frank and Joe's surprise, their stolen camper rested close to the base of the cliff!

"Now who'd do a thing like that?" Joe asked.

"Whoever stole it," Frank commented, "must have realized he couldn't get very far with it."

They glanced about in all directions for possible spies. Frank happened to peer up at the summit of a sheer peak. It was about a mile south of where they stood.

"Look, Joe! There's a flashing light!"

The boys squinted into the afternoon sun at a curious yellow-gold light winking at the top of the mountain.

"Somebody's using a mirror signal," Joe said.

"Signaling who?"

"The guys who stole our camper, maybe?"

"Could be."

Joe turned and started toward their trailer.

"Wait a minute," Frank warned. "This might be a trap."

Together they cautiously approached the camper. It seemed to be in good condition. As Joe was about to enter, a scraping noise came from above, accompanied by a shower of pebbles.

"Quick!" Frank commanded. "Flat against the cliff!"

They dashed to the rock wall, pressing themselves against the cool stone.

The sound grew louder and clods of earth pelted down. Then a huge dead tree crashed and splintered on the ground. It missed Frank and Joe by a foot, but the twisted branches cut deep ridges into the camper.

"You were right, Frank! It was a trap!"

"We'll spring a trap of our own." Frank muttered. "Let's go!"

They worked their way along the base of the precipice, finally reaching the wooded slope adjoining the cliff.

Looking up, Frank said, "We'll circle around and approach them from the rear."

Moving carefully so as not to make any noise, the boys crawled up the slope, using the dense foliage for cover. When they were about thirty feet from the top, something moved in the bushes near the cliff edge.

On their stomachs Frank and Joe inched ahead, pulses pounding with excitement. Soon they were within earshot of two hiding figures.

One said hoarsely, "Look, I'm a thief, not a strong-arm man."

"Same here," said the other. "I don't like this heavy work."

There was silence for a few moments, then the

first man said, "I wish they'd show themselves again so we could bop them. Mungo, take this big rock!"

Mungo! The man who had been trailing the white cabin cruiser! Frank and Joe recognized the speaker's voice as Farkus'.

At Frank's signal, the young detectives let out piercing war whoops and sprang up. The two men wheeled around, their eyes as big as saucers. The Hardys leaped upon them, pinning them to the ground inches from the edge of the cliff.

"Don't! Please don't throw us over!" Mungo pleaded.

"Wait a minute!" Farkus cried out. "We didn't want to do this!"

The boys dragged the men to their feet, bound their wrists with some rope Joe had in his pocket, and marched them down the slope. Their captives stumbled and fell. When they pulled themselves up again, they begged for mercy.

"We'll cooperate, we'll do anything you want!" said Farkus.

"That's right," Mungo added as they reached the turnout. "We're fed up with working for Lasher!"

"How did you get here? Where's your car?" Frank asked the men.

The pair motioned to a spot a hundred yards distant. Their automobile was hidden in a shel-

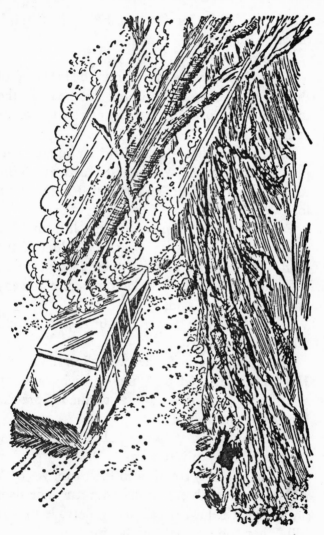

A huge tree crashed down

tered glen. While Joe watched the captives, Frank drove it back to the camper.

"You're coming with us," said Joe.

The prisoners were shoved into the back seat of the Hardys' car. Then Frank hitched on the camper and drove off. Joe chauffered the other vehicle.

An amazed Chet Morton and an equally surprised Biff Hooper watched the arrival of the strange caravan. They had returned minutes before.

Frank ran their camper up the hill and Joe parked the swindlers' car on the shoulder of the road. Then the boys pulled their prisoners out.

"I suppose you want a lawyer before you say anything," Frank said.

"Don't need any lawyers," Mungo said. "We'll tell you all about it."

He explained that Lasher wanted to silence the Hardys. Farkus had told him of their campsite and Lasher had worked out a scheme to lure the boys away and injure them.

"You can tell that to the police," Frank said. "We're taking you into town."

But before they could push their captives back into the convertible, they heard a car door slam on the road below. A park ranger strode up the hill. They had not met him before.

"Hello, boys," he said. "I see you found a good camping spot. Don't forget to wet down all fires."

Then his glance fell upon the bound wrists of the captives. "What's going—?"

"Help us! We've been kidnapped!" Mungo cried out.

"We demand our civil rights!" Farkus added. "Arrest these kids!"

The boys looked at one another in amazement. Biff said, "Why, you crooks! You're the ones who should be arrested!"

"Don't believe a word they say," Farkus bellowed. "See how they got us tied up!"

The park ranger was in a quandary. "I can't take anybody's side," he said. "How do I know who's telling the truth?" He pulled a knife from his pocket and cut the bonds.

"They'll escape!" Chet protested.

"You're the ones who'll run away," Farkus barked.

"Nobody's going to run away," the ranger said. "You all are coming with me to Snowcap."

Mungo and Farkus seemed willing enough. Farkus was to drive their car. The ranger told Mungo to get into the forest service car. Biff set his bike beside the camper and joined Frank, Joe, and Chet in the convertible.

Chet fumed at the thought of how the pair had duped the officer. "What liars! It's a wonder they didn't say they were Smokey the Bear and his brother!"

As they entered the town, Frank exclaimed,

"Hey, we're in luck! There's a State Police car!"

The ranger pulled up behind it, stepped out, and spoke to the trooper. The Hardys joined him and told their side of the story.

"Those men are mixed up with a ring of credit-card counterfeiters," Frank said. "And we can prove it!"

"You mean you know someone who can identify them as swindlers?" the trooper asked.

"Yes." Frank told about Burn, the jeweler who had been bilked. The State Police officer agreed to take Farkus and Mungo to the store.

The suspects were silent as the group walked toward Burn's shop. While Biff, Chet, and the ranger waited outside, Frank and Joe accompanied the officer into the store with Farkus and Mungo. Burn looked up in surprise from a gem he was examining. A young woman assistant disappeared into the back of the store.

The trooper said, "I understand, Mr. Burn, you accepted a fake Magnacard recently."

"That's right."

"Did either of these men present it to you?"

Farkus and Mungo stood before the counter, looking tense.

The jeweler studied them carefully. Then he said, "No. I've never seen these men before!"

CHAPTER XVIII

The Vampire Cave

DISMAYED by the reply, the Hardys faced the jeweler. "But—but you told us about John Minks and—" Joe began.

"I told you nothing!" Burn's mouth turned down and a look of defiance came into his slitted eyes. "Now why don't you go away and stop bothering me!"

The police officer put a hand on the boy's shoulder. "As you can see, it's a case of mistaken identity. We all make a boo-boo now and then."

"But I tell you," Joe persisted, "it's not a mistake!"

Frank nudged his brother. "We can't get anywhere without Burn's help. Protesting won't do any good. Let's go!"

"And let these guys go scot-free?" Joe demanded.

"Listen to your brother," the officer advised. "You haven't got a case here."

Joe realized that the officer was right. Without proof, there was no way to take the criminals into custody.

Frank and Joe joined their friends outside. Chet and Biff were amazed to see Mungo and Farkus walk out and amble down the street.

"What happened?" Biff asked. "You had those crooks dead to rights!"

"The jeweler copped out on us," Frank said. "There's something real fishy behind all this, and we're going to find out what it is."

Biff said, "Of course it's possible that Farkus was not the man who used the Minks Magnacard."

"Theoretically, yes," Frank replied. "But I've watched the jeweler and he acted funny. I'm sure it was Farkus." He asked Chet and Biff to follow the two men.

"Joe and I will keep an eye on the jewelry shop," he said. "I think Burn will react fairly soon. We'll meet you later at the campsite."

Biff and Chet hastened to the Hardys' convertible and drove slowly after the suspects. The men hopped into their own car, accelerated quickly, and headed in the direction of Denver.

"Come on, Biff. Can't you get this heap to go any faster?" Chet complained.

Biff had the pedal down to the floor as they ascended the steep mountain road. It curved sharply and the suspects' car disappeared from sight.

Rounding the curve, the boys saw a road repairman waving a red flag. Biff hit the brakes. Up ahead a power roller was repairing one side of the highway and traffic was alternating, a dozen cars at a time in each direction.

Mungo and Farkus' car had been the last to get through!

Biff and Chet chafed at the delay. Vehicles came from the opposite side in single file. A large trailer was proceeding extra-cautiously.

"Why doesn't he step on it?" Biff fumed.

Finally the last car had passed and the boys were given the go signal. Biff eased slowly past the roller. Once in the clear, he tromped on the gas. But no matter how fast he went, they could not get a glimpse of the other car.

Chet observed. "They must be miles ahead of us by now. We'll never catch 'em, Biff."

"You're right. We might as well go back."

Meanwhile, Frank and Joe were carefully concealed in a doorway, watching the jewelry store in Snowcap.

Finally their vigil was rewarded. The jeweler stepped out and looked up and down the street. Then he set off at a rapid gait and crossed the road. The boys followed.

"He's really got something on his mind!" Frank thought.

Turning a corner, the man headed toward the second house on the left. After opening the front door with a key he disappeared inside.

Joe and Frank crept around to the back yard.
The young sleuths worked their way to the rear
porch. Through an open window they heard a
chair scuff against the floor as Burn sat down.

Then came the dialing of the telephone. After
a few seconds, Burn said, "Pick? . . . Listen.
Those big-money fakers are still around, but I
couldn't get my hands on them!"

There was silence for a few seconds.

Then the jeweler continued, "I could have
grabbed two of them, but the fuzz interfered. I
think they skipped town."

Again only silence, then an exclamation,
"What? . . . You've got them? . . . Up the trail
tonight? . . . But those Hardys are still poking
around . . . Where? . . . The Vampire Cave
. . . Okay."

The phone clicked in its cradle. Moments later
the front door slammed.

Peering around the side of the house, the Hardys saw Burn striding up the street. Apparently
he was returning to his shop.

"What did you make of all that?" Joe asked excitedly.

"Maybe the credit-card thieves were caught!"

"By Pick's gang?"

"I'm beginning to think so."

The boys pondered the new turn of events.
Were two gangs battling each other?

"This mystery is turning out in reverse!" said

Joe. "The other gang—the guys who are after the Magnacard crooks—must be up on Vampire Trail!"

"And tonight's the showdown!" said Frank.

"The moment of truth is at hand." Joe grinned.

As the Hardys walked back to the main street, trying to get a lift to their campsite, Chet and Biff rode by and stopped. They were chagrined by their failure to keep on the trail of the Magnacard fakers. But when Frank and Joe told them the result of the stakeout, they regained their optimism.

"Boy, that'll be a great show!" Biff said.

"Maybe they'll knock each other off," Chet chortled. "Then we won't have so much work to do."

They decided to return to their trailer tent and lay a plan of action. As they neared Blackfoot Meadow campground, Chet said, "Let's visit Prince Cuthbert and see if he's had any news from the police about those sapphire thieves."

The boys were surprised to find that Cuthbert's psychedelic trailer was not in its place. They got out of the car and queried the neighbors.

"Oh, the prince?" said one. "He left."

"Did he say where he was going?" Frank asked.

"No. He just hitched up the trailer to his old jalopy and chugged off."

"He seemed mighty disturbed, that's all I can say," someone else added.

"Gosh," Chet said, "he didn't even say good-by to us."

"You kind of liked that old eccentric, didn't you?" Biff asked.

"He wasn't so bad."

Joe, however, still felt that Cuthbert was suspect. "I don't think we've seen the last of him," he stated as they returned to their car.

After an early supper the boys formulated plans for their hike up Vampire Trail. Sherlock would be tied to the camper with enough food and water to last at least twenty-four hours.

"Silence is essential," Frank declared. "We don't know how many of those crooks might be lurking along the trail. Use your flashlight sparingly, and if it's necessary to say anything, whisper it."

As soon as darkness fell, Frank and Joe took one side of the path, Chet and Biff the other. The stony, tortuous trail tested both their strength and agility. Clouds obscured the moon and the resulting jet-black darkness made the climb even more difficult. They pressed ahead, giving a winking signal now and then to mark their positions.

About halfway to the top of the mountain they halted and had a whispered conference.

"Let's lie in wait for a while," Joe suggested. "If anyone comes up the trail tonight, he'll have to go right past here and we can grab him."

Frank interposed, "Only let's not grab anybody.

The idea is to follow him to his gang's headquarters."

They returned to their positions and waited. Suddenly Chet gave a cry of alarm. Almost at the same instant something fluttered close to the Hardys' heads.

"For Pete's sake!" Joe hissed. "Keep quiet!" He and Frank hastened to Chet's side.

"The bats!" Chet moaned. "One of them almost brushed against my ear. Sorry, fellows."

"*Sh,*" Frank warned. "I hear something."

Far down the path came the sound of footsteps, then a mélange of angry voices.

"You shut up," one said harshly.

"I'll take this case to the Supreme Court!"

"That's Farkus," Joe said.

Another voice, which the Hardys identified as Burn's the jeweler, sneered, "Supreme Court? You'll see your supreme creator first!"

"You can't do this to us. It's illegal!" It was Mungo speaking.

"Look who's talking about legality," someone said with a laugh.

The boys crouched low alongside the trail as the men passed them. Frank could have reached out and touched one who said in a whining tone, "We'll give you anything. Anything you want, but let us go!"

"Lasher, you've had it. The end of the trail will be the end of your crooked career."

The voices trailed off. When they became inaudible, the boys whispered again.

"Just as we thought," Frank said. "It's gang against gang. The guys who hold Vampire Trail have caught the Magnacard crooks!"

They walked up the center of the trail with Joe as lead man. When they came to a steep defile, they stopped for a moment and listened. The mountain was ominously still.

"Okay," Joe said. "The road's clear."

They pressed on single file through the narrow passage which opened onto ground less steep.

"We must be right near the top," Frank said.

Again they heard voices. Crawling on their stomachs, the boys made their way to the edge of a small amphitheater which nature had cut into the mountaintop.

"A great hiding place!" Joe whispered.

"Right," Frank said. "Completely hidden from below."

They crept closer for a better look. In the middle of the amphitheater a small fire was burning. A knot of men were gathered around it. Pick was doing the talking. His voice came through deep and booming.

"Nobody's going to cheat us and get away with it! You swindled Burn!"

"But we'll give you anything," Lasher pleaded. "All the dough we made in the credit-card racket. I've got it hidden. It's all yours. Just let us go!"

"You had your chance to pay when you bought the sapphire," Pick said. "Now you're going to pay—in a different way!"

The Hardys strained their eyes trying to identify the others standing in the flickering firelight. They could make out the terrified faces of Mungo and Farkus, whose jowls were quivering with fear.

Suddenly one of Pick's henchmen whispered something to him and he stopped censuring his captives. With a gesture toward the inky black night he said in a voice dripping with mock kindness:

"You kids can come out of hiding now. All of you are my prisoners!"

CHAPTER XIX

Then There Were Three

PICK's words hit the boys like a bucket of ice water! Was this a bluff meant to dislodge them from their hiding place? How had they been discovered on their trek up Vampire Trail? They crouched, every muscle tense.

There was a rustling in the bushes behind them. Frank, Chet, and Biff spun around to look. But Joe, falling flat to the ground, slithered off in an effort to escape.

Just then a powerful beam of light flashed into the eyes of the trio. Two men carrying rifles appeared. "Okay, you guys. On your feet. Reach for the stars!"

There was nothing to do but obey.

It was only when they stood up that Frank became aware of Joe's absence. "Good boy," he thought. Joe's escape was the only hope for rescue!

The three were escorted to the fire, gun muzzles prodding them in the back. As they approached, they got a better look at Pick.

His high forehead was crowned by disheveled blond hair. His eyes looked green in the flickering firelight, which threw sinister shadows on his pocked face. His stubbly chin was thrust out defiantly.

"Only three! I said there would be four!" Pick yelled to the guards.

"We found only three," one of the men replied.

"So I see!" Pick's eyes blazed. "You—the other boy—come out of your hiding place! There's not a chance of you getting away. My men have been spying on you kids for the last half hour."

In a lower voice he told the three captives, "The trail is tightly guarded and the only way out is a sheer drop of a thousand feet over that rock wall."

The trio remained silent.

Pick glanced at his wrist watch and again bellowed, "Every minute you hide out will mean that much more time in the bat cave!"

"The bat cave? What's that?" Frank spoke up.

"Pretty curious, aren't you?" said Pick. "Curiosity killed a cat, and it's going to kill a lot more!"

"In that case," Biff put in, "you've nothing to lose if you tell us what this is all about."

"Yes," said Chet. "After all, we don't want to die ignorant."

Pick let out a yell of delight. "Ignorant? You all were pretty ignorant to come snooping around here. What are your names?"

The boys told him.

"The other Hardy kid is the one that's missing," Pick said to his men.

"That's Joe," Lasher volunteered, groveling for favor.

"Shut up!" Pick glowered at the man, then turned his attention back to Chet.

"Some people are just born unlucky," he said. "But since you want to know all about it, I'll tell you."

He went into a long discourse, waving his arms and punctuating the strange story with sarcastic bursts of laughter.

He and his men were engaged in the illegal mining of sapphires. They had discovered an abandoned digging on land which was now government property. The only way up to the mine, outside of scaling the cliff, was by Vampire Trail.

"So we waylaid unwelcome campers," Pick said, "and scared everybody off."

"With your vampire bats," said Frank. "But they only live in Central America!"

Pick gave a gleeful laugh that reverberated through the rock-walled clearing. "I got them from a buddy of mine in Nicaragua. Smuggled them into the country."

In one part of the mine, he said, there was a thermal cave, where bats could live comfortably. Occasionally he let some of them out on the trail to frighten people away, but the poor mammals died quickly when exposed to the cold mountain air.

"But what about the marks on our necks?" Chet asked.

"First we bopped you kids, then nipped you with a pair of pliers."

"Look, Pick, why don't you let us go?" Frank said. "We were only out to get those credit-card crooks." The young detective was trying to stall for time so Joe would have a chance to get help. "Incidentally, what's your beef with them, and what about Fingers' gang?" he asked.

"Now that's quite a story," the gang leader replied. He explained that Elkin Burn, the town jeweler, was one of the outlets for his sapphires. The Terrible Trio had helped him work the mine but had been caught stealing so he fired them.

"Pick, we don't have a grudge against you," Frank said.

"I'm sorry, kid, truly sorry."

"Then you'll let us go?" Chet asked.

"Of course not." A savage look came into the man's eyes. "You know too much. Sometimes the innocent must suffer with the guilty."

"Meaning what?" Frank asked.

"I'll have to drop you all into the flooded mine shaft. But first Mr. Lasher goes into the bat cave."

"Don't, please!" Lasher begged, crawling over to Pick.

The miner gave him a kick. "Get out of here, you crumb! You double-crossed Burn with that phony credit card. Now you're going to get it!"

Lasher pleaded, "Let me go! I can make a lot more money with those credit cards. I'll turn it all over to you!"

"Too late!" Pick said. "You're going in with the bats!"

"But I can't stand bats!" Lasher cried. "They drive me crazy!"

"Good!"

Lasher sprang up and made a dash toward the edge of the clearing. A gun barrel was smacked hard against the back of his neck and he fell in a heap.

"Don't put him in the bat cave until he recovers," Pick ordered. "We'll play the rest of our little game after we catch Joe Hardy."

When Joe had heard Pick's first threat he had unstrapped his rucksack and crawled toward the edge of the cliff. He lay in the tall grass, praying that no one would find him. If there were only some way down!

In the light of the moon which now shone through a rift in the heavy clouds, he could see that there was no means of escape, except perhaps with mountain-climbing gear.

As Joe peered down into the abyss a tiny point of light caught his eye. Eagerly he leaned over as far as he could without falling off. A small fire glowed at the base of the cliff.

"A campfire!" Joe thought. "If I only could attract the attention of whoever's there!"

He picked up a few pebbles and dropped them over the cliff. Then he covered himself with brush and tall grass, hoping that Pick's men would not discover him.

Joe fell into a deep sleep. When he awakened, the sun was rising. He peered over the cliff and was amazed by what he saw.

A mountain climber was halfway up the rock wall! He was using pitons and every available handhold.

The man lifted his head and Joe recognized him immediately. *Fritz Burger!*

Still half concealed, the boy beckoned. Burger saw him and Joe motioned the Austrian to be silent.

At the same time one of Pick's men, who had begun to search again at dawn, was working his way closer to the edge of the cliff. Joe lay perfectly still, watching fearfully through the thick blades of grass.

Methodically the man beat the bushes, coming closer and closer to Joe's hiding place.

"On the next pass," Joe thought, "he'll step right on me!"

Just then a hound bayed in the distance. The searcher stopped and listened. The dog bayed again and the man wheeled around in the direction of the miners' camp.

CHAPTER XX

The Jackpot

FEARING trouble, the guard raced to the camp. His legs flew as he traversed the tall grass and low bushes. Suddenly he stumbled and fell headlong.

Uttering an oath, the man picked himself up and glared at the object he had tripped over. It was a rucksack. Stenciled on it was the name *J. Hardy*.

The man scooped it up. As he approached the camp he saw Sherlock the bloodhound fawning over Biff Hooper.

"Down! Get down, Sherlock!" Biff said.

"So that bloodhound followed you," Pick said to Biff. Seeing the guard running toward him, the gang leader barked, "I told you to find Joe Hardy!"

"He got away, Boss, but I found this!" The man held up Joe's rucksack.

A foxy look came into Pick's eyes and he smiled at the clever thought which crossed his mind.

"Bring that hound here!" he ordered.

Biff took the dog by the collar and led him over to Pick.

The miner held the dog's nose to the rucksack, then said, "Now go and find Joe Hardy!"

Frank and Chet, their eyes bloodshot from an anxious, sleepless night, cried out in protest.

"What's the matter?" Frank said. "Aren't your men clever enough to find my brother without a hound?"

"Maybe not," Pick replied. He added with a sneer, "I think your brother got away—for good!"

"Like falling over the cliff." Burn chortled. "I wouldn't surprise me, Pick."

"We'll find out soon enough," the miner replied. "No need to hurry. Rustle up some chow first."

Pick's men produced a portable stove from inside the tunnel and prepared breakfast.

"Don't we get something, too?" Chet asked.

"You'll have no need for food," Pick retorted with a wicked grin.

"But—but—even a condemned man gets a last meal!"

"The kid's got a point," said Burn.

"What do you say, Lasher?" Pick asked.

The Magnacard swindler turned his ashen face away. His hands trembled.

"Lasher's not hungry," Burn needled. "Neither are his two cronies."

"We are," Frank spoke up. "Make my eggs once over lightly."

"Some spunk these kids have," said Pick.

The three boys ate leisurely, and Frank kept glancing at his watch when all had finished. Pick wiped his greasy hands on his shirt and announced that the search for Joe Hardy would be renewed.

"Sherlock will lead us to him," he said. Tying a rope around the dog's collar, he let the canine sniff around the area. Finally Sherlock picked up the trail.

With Pick beckoning to them devilishly, the boys followed the dog toward the edge of the cliff.

Sherlock strained at the rope and walked right up to the rim. Frank's stomach felt like a lead weight. Had Joe fallen into the abyss during the night? Suddenly he spied two objects on the ground close to the cliff edge. He knelt down to shield the spot from the view of Pick and his men.

Biff, too, had seen the piton and the ring! Devices used by mountain climbers! Frank realized that Joe had miraculously escaped. Now they must play for time until help could arrive!

"Say your prayers if you want," Pick said and turned to his henchmen. "One less Hardy boy to deal with." Then he snarled, "Okay, bring 'em all back. We'll finish the elimination."

The three prisoners were prodded to the camp,

where Lasher, Mungo, and Farkus sat around in dejected silence. A shout came from one of the men who had been guarding the approach to the miners' camp. He marched up the trail pushing a disheveled figure before him.

"Prince Cuthbert!" Chet called out in amazement.

The prince's helmet crown was askew and his robes were tattered. Chet and Frank hurried to his side.

"Chet—and Frank! I thought I'd never find you. Where's Joe?"

"Never mind the gab," Pick cried out. "Who is this nut?"

"Sir?" Cuthbert squared his shoulders and looked Pick straight in the eye. "I came to say good-by to my friends. I set off hoping to avoid a tearful farewell, but turned my caravan about."

Cuthbert spoke to the boys. "I found your trailer tent with Sherlock guarding it. So I let the poor dog loose hoping he would lead me to you—and so he has!"

Pick's men looked on, smiling and twirling their forefingers at their heads.

"What impudent fellows!" the prince continued. "Let us return to your trailer. A cup of steaming hot tea will be in order."

Chet shook his head in disbelief. "You mean you came all the way back to say good-by to us?"

"Not only that," Cuthbert replied. He thrust his hand inside a satin cummerbund, pulled out a sapphire, and gave it to Frank. "This is a gift for Mrs. Hardy. When Chet told me it was her birthstone I took this sapphire from the pouch and put it in a safe place. Fortunate that I did, otherwise the robbers would have gotten this one too."

"Thanks," Frank said. "You're very thoughtful, Prince."

"Not at all." Cuthbert bowed. "Now will you introduce me to these uncouth friends of yours?"

The gang members laughed heartily at this remark and the prince's face showed his annoyance. "That one looks familiar," he said, pointing to Burn.

"Of course. You're the man who wanted to sell me those sapphires," the jeweler sneered. "Instead, one of Pick's men and I broke into your trailer and got them free."

"Shut up, Burn," Pick growled. "And that goes for this old lunatic, too!"

"Indeed," Cuthbert shot back, curling one of the points of his mustache. "I see you are not used to royalty!"

"So that's it!" Pick said cynically. "You think you're a king or something."

"A prince," Cuthbert corrected him. "Descended from the line of King Arthur."

"Excuse me, Your Highness," Pick said, bowing

mockingly. "We can use some royalty. It might add legality to what we're going to do here."

"And what is that?" asked the prince, straightening his crown.

"An execution! That's what. We'll give a royal execution to these three kids and Lasher's crew. Now, won't that make it legal?"

"Please don't hurt the prince!" pleaded Chet.

"Of course not. We'll let him go. Who'd believe his babblings, anyhow?"

"Desist," Cuthbert said, "or my archers will fall upon you, not to mention my knights in armor!"

In a low voice Frank said, "Keep it up, Prince. We need as much time as possible."

Cuthbert turned on him coldly. "You don't believe me?"

"Well," Frank said quietly, "I thought you were kid—"

"Cut the nonsense," Pick interrupted. He motioned to his men. "Lasher goes to the bat cave right now."

Two of the miners seized the swindler, who began screaming and kicking as he was carried into the tunnel. His wails of anguish were fading in the distance when three shots rang out in quick succession.

"Don't move. Drop your guns and stay where you are!" The strident voice came over a bullhorn and five State Police officers appeared. Behind them was Joe Hardy.

"Joe!" Chet cried in relief.

Pick's eyes popped and his jaw dropped as if he were looking at a ghost. His guards threw their guns to the ground.

With Joe was the Austrian mountain climber, Burger. Frank realized what had happened. Burger had rescued Joe!

"Search the tunnel! Hurry!" Frank cried out, pointing.

One of the troopers hurried forward, pistol drawn. He returned a few minutes later with the two guards and Lasher.

Pick was tight-lipped, but his inner fury showed in his blazing eyes. Finally he blurted, "You Hardys ruined my racket!"

"And the Magnacard caper, too," one of the troopers said, while the others were rounding up the prisoners. They were all advised of their rights.

Mungo and Farkus readily admitted their guilt in the credit-card swindles. Whip Lasher made a full confession. He admitted that it was he who had followed the Hardys in the beginning of their camping trip and had let the air out of their tires.

"A real prankster," one of the troopers commented. "Well, you won't be playing any tricks for a long time to come."

It was Lasher, too, who had fire-bombed the boys' camper. Farkus had been with Lasher at the Mountain Dogie Store.

Just then a report came in over the police portable radio which one of the troopers was carrying. The Terrible Trio had returned to Denver and had been picked up. They were being charged with malicious mischief. Mungo's pals at the Badland Reservoir Marina headquarters had also been arrested.

Joe Hardy apologized to Prince Cuthbert for suspecting that he had any connection with the criminals.

Chet was very superior about it. "Can't you tell a good guy when you see one?" he asked.

"Thank you, Chet," Cuthbert said with a broad smile. "Now I must wend my way through the mountains. My travels eventually will carry me back to the land of my ancestors."

The police looked on in amazement as the eccentric shook hands with the boys and took his leave.

"Be sure to give my compliments to your dear mother," the prince called over his shoulder.

Frank fingered the sapphire in his pocket and promised to convey the message.

The handcuffed prisoners were marched down Vampire Trail and put into State Police cars.

As the four boys walked to their camper, Joe asked, "All set to go home now?"

"Go home?" Biff exclaimed. "Why, we've hardly started our camping trip!"

"That's right," Chet added. "I vote for a little

more fishing. And don't forget, we have some reward money to split up."

"You're right on both counts," Frank said. "I'll telephone Dad and tell him we solved the case. Get lunch ready, Chet. Joe and I will go to Blackfoot Meadow to make the call."

As the Hardys rode off on the motorbike, Biff scratched Sherlock's ears. "I'm glad the mystery of Vampire Trail has been solved, old boy," he said.

But the carefree days which followed proved to be only a short respite for Frank and Joe. Almost immediately upon their return home, they would be faced with another challenging mystery, *The Masked Monkey*.

ORDER FORM

BOBBSEY TWINS™
ADVENTURE SERIES

by Laura Lee Hope

Now that you've met the Bobbsey Twins, we're sure you'll want to "accompany" them
their exciting adventures. So for your convenience, we've enclosed this handy order fo

49 TITLES AT YOUR BOOKSELLE
OR COMPLETE AND MAIL THIS
HANDY COUPON TO:

GROSSET & DUNLAP, INC.
P.O. Box 941, Madison Square Post Office, New York, N.Y. 10010

Please send me the Bobbsey Twins™ Adventure Book(s) checked below @ $2.95 each, p
50¢ *per book* postage and handling. My check or money order for $_____ is enclos

☐	1. Of Lakeport	8001-X	☐	48. On A Bicycle Trip	804
☐	2. Adventure in the Country	8002-8	☐	49. Own Little Ferryboat	804
☐	3. Secret at the Seashore	8003-6	☐	50. At Pilgrim Rock	805
☐	4. Mystery at School	8004-4	☐	51. Forest Adventure	805
☐	5. At Snow Lodge	8005-2	☐	52. At London Tower	80
☐	6. On A Houseboat	8006-0	☐	53. In the Mystery Cave	805
☐	7. Mystery at Meadowbrook	8007-9	☐	54. In Volcano Land	805
☐	8. Big Adventure at Home	8008-7	☐	55. And the Goldfish Mystery	805
☐	9. Search in the Great City	8009-5	☐	56. And the Big River Mystery	805
☐	10. On Blueberry Island	8010-9	☐	57. The Greek Hat Mystery	805
☐	11. Mystery on the Deep Blue Sea	8011-7	☐	58. Search for the Green Rooster	805
☐	12. Adventure in Washington	8012-5	☐	59. And Their Camel Adventure	80
☐	13. Visit to the Great West	8013-3	☐	60. Mystery of the King's Puppet	80
☐	14. And the Cedar Camp Mystery	8014-1	☐	61. Secret of Candy Castle	80
☐	15. And the County Fair Mystery	8015-X	☐	62. And the Doodlebug Mystery	80
☐	16. Camping Out	8016-8	☐	63. And the Talking Fox Mystery	806
☐	17. Adventures With Baby May	8017-6	☐	64. The Red, White and Blue Mystery	80
☐	18. And the Play House Secret	8018-4	☐	65. Dr. Funnybone's Secret	80
☐	19. And the Four-Leaf Clover Mystery	8019-2	☐	66. The Tagalong Giraffe	80
			☐	67. And the Flying Clown	80
☐	20. The Mystery at Cherry Corners	8020-6	☐	68. On The Sun-Moon Cruise	80
☐	24. Wonderful Winter Secret	8024-9	☐	69. The Freedom Bell Mystery	80
☐	25. And the Circus Surprise	8025-7	☐	70. And the Smoky Mountain Mystery	80
☐	27. Solve A Mystery	8027-3	☐	71. In a TV Mystery	80
☐	47. At Big Bear Pond	8047-8	☐	72. The Coral Turtle Mystery	80

SHIP TO:
NAME _____

(please print)

ADDRESS _____

CITY _____ STATE _____ ZIP _____

Printed in U.S.A.   **Please do not send ca**

ORDER FORM

HARDY BOYS
MYSTERY STORIES®
by Franklin W. Dixon

that you've met Frank and Joe Hardy, we're sure you'll want to read the thrilling books
e *Hardy Boys* ● adventure series.
To make it easy for you to own all the books in this exciting series, we've enclosed
handy order form.

59 TITLES AT YOUR BOOKSELLER OR
MPLETE THIS HANDY COUPON AND MAIL TO:

SSET & DUNLAP, INC.
3ox 941, Madison Square Post Office, New York, N.Y. 10010

e send me the *Hardy Boys*® books checked below. My check or money order for $_____ is enclosed
ncludes 50¢ *per book* postage and handling. (Please *do not* send cash.)

Hardy Boys Mystery Stories® @ $2.95 each:

<table>
<tr><td>Tower Treasure</td><td>8901-7</td><td>☐ 30.</td><td>Wailing Siren Mystery</td><td>8930-0</td></tr>
<tr><td>House on the Cliff</td><td>8902-5</td><td>☐ 31.</td><td>Secret of Wildcat Swamp</td><td>8931-9</td></tr>
<tr><td>Secret of the Old Mill</td><td>8903-3</td><td>☐ 32.</td><td>Crisscross Shadow</td><td>8932-7</td></tr>
<tr><td>Missing Chums</td><td>8904-1</td><td>☐ 33.</td><td>The Yellow Feather Mystery</td><td>8933-5</td></tr>
<tr><td>Hunting for Hidden Gold</td><td>8905-X</td><td>☐ 34.</td><td>The Hooded Hawk Mystery</td><td>8934-3</td></tr>
<tr><td>Shore Road Mystery</td><td>8906-8</td><td>☐ 35.</td><td>The Clue in the Embers</td><td>8935-1</td></tr>
<tr><td>Secret of the Caves</td><td>8907-8</td><td>☐ 36.</td><td>The Secrets of Pirates Hill</td><td>8936-X</td></tr>
<tr><td>Mystery of Cabin Island</td><td>8908-4</td><td>☐ 37.</td><td>Ghost at Skeleton Rock</td><td>8937-8</td></tr>
<tr><td>Great Airport Mystery</td><td>8909-2</td><td>☐ 38.</td><td>Mystery at Devil's Paw</td><td>8938-6</td></tr>
<tr><td>What Happened At Midnight</td><td>8910-6</td><td>☐ 39.</td><td>Mystery of the Chinese Junk</td><td>8939-4</td></tr>
<tr><td>While the Clock Ticked</td><td>8911-4</td><td>☐ 40.</td><td>Mystery of the Desert Giant</td><td>8940-8</td></tr>
<tr><td>Footprints Under the Window</td><td>8912-2</td><td>☐ 41.</td><td>Clue of the Screeching Owl</td><td>8941-6</td></tr>
<tr><td>Mark on the Door</td><td>8913-0</td><td>☐ 42.</td><td>Viking Symbol Mystery</td><td>8942-4</td></tr>
<tr><td>Hidden Harbor Mystery</td><td>8914-9</td><td>☐ 43.</td><td>Mystery of the Aztec Warrior</td><td>8943-2</td></tr>
<tr><td>Sinister Sign Post</td><td>8915-7</td><td>☐ 44.</td><td>Haunted Fort</td><td>8944-0</td></tr>
<tr><td>A Figure in Hiding</td><td>8916-6</td><td>☐ 45.</td><td>Mystery of the Spiral Bridge</td><td>8945-9</td></tr>
<tr><td>Secret Warning</td><td>8917-3</td><td>☐ 46.</td><td>Secret Agent on Flight 101</td><td>8946-7</td></tr>
<tr><td>Twisted Claw</td><td>8918-1</td><td>☐ 47.</td><td>Mystery of the Whale Tattoo</td><td>8947-5</td></tr>
<tr><td>Disappearing Floor</td><td>8919-X</td><td>☐ 48.</td><td>The Arctic Patrol Mystery</td><td>8948-3</td></tr>
<tr><td>Mystery of the Flying Express</td><td>8920-3</td><td>☐ 49.</td><td>The Bombay Boomerang</td><td>8949-1</td></tr>
<tr><td>The Clue of the Broken Blade</td><td>8921-1</td><td>☐ 50.</td><td>Danger on Vampire Trail</td><td>8950-5</td></tr>
<tr><td>The Flickering Torch Mystery</td><td>8922-X</td><td>☐ 51.</td><td>The Masked Monkey</td><td>8951-3</td></tr>
<tr><td>Melted Coins</td><td>8923-3</td><td>☐ 52.</td><td>The Shattered Helmet</td><td>8952-3</td></tr>
<tr><td>Short-Wave Mystery</td><td>8924-6</td><td>☐ 53.</td><td>The Clue of the Hissing Serpent</td><td>8953-X</td></tr>
<tr><td>Secret Panel</td><td>8925-4</td><td>☐ 54.</td><td>The Mysterious Caravan</td><td>8954-8</td></tr>
<tr><td>The Phantom Freighter</td><td>8926-2</td><td>☐ 55.</td><td>The Witchmaster's Key</td><td>8955-6</td></tr>
<tr><td>Secret of Skull Mountain</td><td>8927-0</td><td>☐ 56.</td><td>The Jungle Pyramid</td><td>8956-4</td></tr>
<tr><td>The Sign of the Crooked Arrow</td><td>8928-9</td><td>☐ 57.</td><td>The Firebird Rocket</td><td>8957-2</td></tr>
<tr><td>The Secret of the Lost Tunnel</td><td>8929-7</td><td>☐ 58.</td><td>The Sting of The Scorpion</td><td>8958-0</td></tr>
</table>

Also Available: ☐ The Hardy Boys Detective Handbook @ $3.95   1990-6

r'O: _____

_____
(please print)

SS _____

_____ STATE _____ ZIP _____

In U.S.A.   **Please do not send cash.**